SUMMER SKATE

ALSO BY SEAN AVERY

Ice Capades: A Memoir of Fast Living and Tough Hockey

ALSO BY LESLIE COHEN

This Love Story Will Self-Destruct
My Ride or Die

SUMMER SKATE

A Novel

SEAN AVERY AND
LESLIE COHEN

BenBella Books, Inc.
Dallas, TX

Summer Skate copyright © 2025 by Sean Avery and Leslie Cohen

All rights reserved. Except in the case of brief quotations embodied in critical articles or reviews, no part of this book may be used or reproduced, stored, transmitted, or used in any manner whatsoever, including for training artificial intelligence (AI) technologies or for automated text and data mining, without prior written permission from the publisher.

BenBella Books, Inc.
8080 N. Central Expressway
Suite 1700
Dallas, TX 75206
benbellabooks.com
Send feedback to feedback@benbellabooks.com

BenBella is a federally registered trademark.

Printed in the United States of America
10 9 8 7 6 5 4 3 2 1

Library of Congress Control Number: 2025016182
ISBN 9781637747315 (trade paperback)
ISBN 9781637747322 (electronic)

Editing by Elizabeth Smith and Leah Wilson
Copyediting by Karen Wise
Proofreading by Jenny Bridges and Cheryl Beacham
Text design and composition by Aaron Edmiston
Cover design by Sarah Avinger
Cover image © Adobe Stock / Vladislav
Printed by Lake Book Manufacturing

Special discounts for bulk sales are available.
Please contact bulkorders@benbellabooks.com.

1

CARTER

Durham, New Hampshire, two years ago

IT'S A SNOWY NIGHT IN A town that is all activity and cheer, even after a loss. The cobblestone streets are blanketed in white and lined with twinkling Christmas trees. I have my red-cheeked girlfriend under my arm as we walk down the street, the tails of her scarf flying in the icy wind. We walk past a bar with its door open. An amateur band is playing "Take Me Home, Country Roads." It's eleven thirty on a Saturday night and we're headed back to my apartment, off campus. She's got my jacket on.

We turn onto a street that's quiet. We hear only the sound of our boots on the sleeted pavement, the crunch of salt under our feet. Three big guys with beards walk toward us. Townies. They're drunk.

One of them looks at her and asks, "How does it feel to be with the biggest bitch on campus?"

Clearly, they watched me take that bad penalty at the end of the game. It cost my team the win. And while I can't erase the past, I can predict the future. I know exactly what's about to happen. Everything goes into slow motion.

I turn to my girlfriend, very calmly, and say, "Don't ask any questions. Just turn around and walk home, okay? Right now. Go."

I am clear. I am strategic. This is when I do my best computing. In the eye of the storm. If I could choose to live in this space, I would. It's where I feel comfortable. Serviceable. On the team, this is my role. I cause chaos. For distraction. For intimidation. For the win. I've done it since I was a kid.

"Who did you just call a bitch?" I say.

Before he can answer, I smack one guy. Open-hand slap across the jaw. He's down. I hit the second guy on the side of his head, on his ear, before his hands even come out of his pockets. He's down. The third guy is six feet away, coming toward me. I take two hard steps and bury my shoulder into his belly button, wrap my arms around his legs and pick him up off the ground and slam him on his head. Bounce his head right off the concrete. He's out cold. Bleeding from his ears.

I sit down on the curb. I have blood on my hands, but they aren't shaking.

At least there were three. It's easier to sell.

I take out my phone, put my hand on one guy's chest to see if he's still breathing. I call the cops.

"Hi. My name is Carter Hughes. I play hockey for the University of New Hampshire. I just got attacked by three men on the corner of Summer Street and Main. One of the guys is hurt badly. Send an ambulance and the police. I'll stick around until you get here."

2

JESSICA

New York City, present day

I GET UP WITH THE SUN, which I've never done before, in any prior stage of life. But once you have children, suddenly you're a confused but obedient farmer, ready to plow the fucking fields of the Upper East Side. You see, they'll be awake soon, *the children*, and I've learned that I have to do a significant amount of yoga plus a cold plunge in which I'm hoping some form of baptism occurs, before I have the power to deal with them.

So, I take my preparatory measures. Is that sweat dropping onto my yoga mat, or tears? Depends on the morning.

By 6:45, my time is up. My five-year-old daughter is awake, making demands. I start by getting her dressed for school, shoving clothes onto her while she's flopping on the bed like a fish. She could not be less helpful if she were doing it on purpose, which she more than likely is. I used to strive for cute outfits, but the bloom is off the rose now and I strive for a look that screams "not in violation of public decency laws."

She takes a solid ten minutes to choose a pair of pants, which turns out to be the only pair of pants that has a hole in it. I tell her no.

"Some clothes are meant to be ripped, Mom! It's *fashion*," she says.

"But these aren't jeans! They're regular pants!"

I let her wear them. What the hell. I don't know what the kids are wearing these days. Maybe it *is* fashion.

I get myself dressed in a T-shirt and leather miniskirt. I don't care how early it is. I'm not showing up to this shit in exercise clothes. The Upper East Side moms have ruined exercise clothes for me. I once went to drop-off in a short black dress and fishnet stockings and one of the moms told me I looked like I had spent the night in Mick Jagger's hotel room. You know what? Nicest thing she's ever said to me.

I hustle my daughter into the kitchen for breakfast, which is sort of like herding a drunk cat that wants nothing to do with you. But I focus. I keep my eye on the prize. If I don't give her constant cheerleading for this harrowing journey, she will go astray or stop altogether.

Do you want yogurt or cereal?

. . .

Yogurt or cereal?

. . .

Answer me, please.

Pancakes!

No. No pancakes. Only on the weekends.

Waffles!

No waffles.

Why?

Why? Because I fear that anything more than a two-step process might break me. So I plead. I bargain. I lodge a bunch of threats against her dearest stuffed animals. "Choose a breakfast or the elephant gets it."

There's crying in the background, which means I must now address my two-year-old, who is wailing from his crib. I will never understand why kids wake up and cry. Imagine, as an adult, the state you would have to be in to wake up from sleeping and head straight into tears. Are they crying because it's over? Because that I might understand.

He's a second child, used to a steady level of neglect. It's part of his lifestyle. So I throw a banana into his cage and he stops.

Good monkey.

The difference between a first child and a second child is that a first child gets toast with butter and jam and the crusts cut off and the second child gets a piece of bread.

By now you may be noticing a distinct lack of a second parent. But he's there. *Oh*, he's there. You see, dads are blessed with the uncanny ability to never hear their children cry. So, he's there but he's in bed, lounging, and one kid could be losing a fucking ear and he will not budge from that spot until something crazy happens, like he himself has to pee. Then, if I'm lucky, he'll take a shower, with vague plans to help me after, once everything is already done.

Having kids is fun! Instead of having morning sex, you fight over who gets to eat breakfast sitting down.

And I want to have sex with my husband. I really do. My husband is Alejandro Martinez. He is extremely hot and hails from Mexico City. He is tall, dark, and handsome but the specific kind of handsome that knows about the South American markets. However, nowadays we spend most of our time together taking care of our children, and during that time we're usually pissing each other off, which does not lend itself to sex.

The baby is crying again.

"He's trying to say something!" my daughter yells from the kitchen.

"What is it?" I reply.

"Help!"

After breakfast, I face my greatest challenge of the morning: getting my daughter to pee before we leave. I once saw an episode of *Euphoria* where the main character was so depressed that she couldn't make it to the bathroom to pee. Couldn't stand up. Couldn't exert the muscles necessary to walk the thirty-five feet to the bathroom. You watch her struggle, crawl on the ground as time collapses to create one endless, suffocating loop, life passing her by as she cries and screams and whimpers. I relate to this.

After peeing, my daughter will attempt to tear apart the house in one final blow to our empire. I don't really care about the bed being made, but I feel a legal responsibility to make sure her rummaging in the drawers doesn't result in a small object on the loose that my son could swallow. He doesn't eat pizza with the slightest speck of green on it, but I'm somehow worried he's going to take down a lithium battery.

The baby is at least partially to blame for my lack of progress at work. Because in case anyone is trying to locate my brain, it's busy keeping track of the various shoes of the dolls in my house, to make sure my son doesn't mistake them for M&M's.

By some miracle, my daughter is in her jacket with the 105 things she needs for a single day of school—her library book that we forgot to read, a rest blanket that they send home to be cleaned once a week, a stuffed animal that also needs to be cleaned. Really. Guys. Not that concerned. This child has licked the hand of our doorman.

Our nanny arrives, ten minutes early, bless her heart, and heads toward the baby. I grab my daughter by the jacket arm and drag her out the door, without saying goodbye to my husband because the water is still running; he's nearing the end of his thirty-minute shower, and I don't want to interrupt the spa session he's been having this morning.

I grab my phone. One missed call from my agent. I take a deep breath. I text him: *I can't talk right now. Call you later.* I slip my phone into my backpack, and we head to the lobby. We have a five-minute walk to school. You'd think I'd be home free. But no. Because that's when the question-and-answer segment of our journey begins.

What is a church?
What kind of people are immune to snake bites?
How much cake will I get on my birthday?
Why is there nighttime?
If grown-ups have babies and kids don't, then who had the first baby?

I tell her: I don't know, ask Daddy, or sometimes just "okay" because I've lost track of whether she's asking or telling. Then, suddenly, she wants a scary story. You want a scary story? Sure. How about this one: Our nanny calls in sick.

As we walk, she is clutching a love letter she wrote to a boy in her class. She is so excited to see what his reaction will be and asking if it is better to give it to him on the street or in his cubby. And with this, I suddenly understand all the romantic problems of the world. Because I've seen the boys in her class. They don't deserve this much consideration. She needs someone more mature. I keep thinking: *Is there a third grader you could give this to?*

At some point between Madison and Park, my daughter has a question about her legs. She stops walking. She decides that she can't walk. Like an idiot, I stop to ask: "What's wrong?" I lean down. She's whispering. After the fourth repetition, I figure it out. She says that when she walks short distances, they don't hurt. But when she walks long distances, they do. I drag us onward. So she has legs. She is in possession of a pair of legs.

We maneuver through the crowd of chatting parents and noisy children. I am holding my daughter's sweaty palm, dragging her forward to the teacher, turning a smile on and off at the parents I know, like a light switch that somebody keeps hitting over and over. I can feel my backpack vibrating, my phone pressed between my shoulders, a shot of stress running through me, because I can't believe he's calling again, after I just sent that message. *It's not even nine a.m.!*

We make it to the door. And more importantly, the teacher. The handoff is about to take place. It feels precarious. Like making sure a bee goes through a keyhole. But then, it happens.

Once she's inside, my hands are free, but my soul is still trapped. The half block between school and the outside world is a minefield. Because now I am faced with another obstacle: the other moms. And not just any moms. The moms who have chosen to stay, to linger, to socialize. And those are by far the worst kinds of moms. There's nothing I respect more than a mom who drops her kid off and then gets the fuck out as quickly as possible.

But they don't care about my respect, just mundane chitchat about the weather, what coat they chose to wear and why, their designer handbags slung over their shoulders. The scene. The *scene*.

"Oh! Jessica! Do you want to join us for a moms' lunch on Friday?"

"Ohhhh, sorry, I can't," I say, kicking off this Oscar-worthy performance with a wince of pain.

"Oh no. Got plans?"

No, I just . . . don't want to.

And then I delve into the details of an emergency dental procedure. I write fiction for a living. Details make all the difference.

We are joined by the moms wearing pleated skirts and wielding tennis rackets. The tennis moms. They're closing in on me.

"Jess! I was thinking that we might be able to get your help with the book fair this year . . . Since you're a writer and all . . . "

"Yeah . . . I don't know. I don't think so."

"The book fair is *such* an important part of the curriculum! It really enriches the children's—"

I look around, as if scanning for surveillance cameras. "Where are we right now that we have to pretend to like the book fair? *We're outside! Nobody can hear us!*

And then I smile because I think this is funny, but judging by their looks, they are horrified. They'll turn to each other once I'm gone and say: "That bitch." But I don't think it was particularly bitchy. I think I showed a great deal of restraint. I could have said, "Thanks, but I'd rather slit my own throat."

I keep walking. Maybe my behavior at drop-off is a detriment to my daughter and her social life at school, but it's a risk I'm willing to take.

Once I make it to the corner, I am free, and there's nothing quite like it. That post-drop-off bliss. Wind in your hair. Freedom coursing through your veins. What can't I do?

One of the dads catches up to me. He's doing his part to avoid the crowd by hoisting a scooter over his head. He once told me that he finds if he carries the scooter over his head and looks pained, people will generally leave him alone. *Gosh, this thing is awfully weighty. I couldn't possibly chitchat.* He's six foot three and was once a star wrestler at Cornell, but yes, he's being conquered by a three-pound scooter. Dads can get away with so much. Nobody even looks at him.

He meets me on the corner, and we agree to walk to the subway together.

"Why do they keep telling us to put the kids in sneakers?" he asks.

"I know. Is somebody sending their child to school in cowboy boots?"

Fifth Avenue is bathed in sun. The sidewalks are empty but for a few joggers, construction workers waiting to be let into buildings, other parents dragging their children along.

We pass by the Guggenheim, then the Met, each empty and

bracing for the day. We walk behind a group of girls in plaid uniforms. We comment on how the misuse of the word *literal* is rampant among the youth of today. We complain about how the school is always sending the kids home with 107-degree fevers. And then at home, magically, their fevers go away.

"They're so annoying on the phone," I say.

"Yeah, and if you don't answer the calls, they're even worse."

I laugh. *Doesn't answer the calls!* I have such admiration for this man. *How has this never occurred to me?*

They have a hard job, we decide. Kids go from totally fine to exorcism to totally fine in the span of one day. Like, I'll wake up one morning thinking I'm going to have a banner day and instead I end up at the pediatrician's office, dedicating an entire day to ear wax. Is it an ear infection or not? Three doctors must weigh in. After the third, I'll start to feel a bit of fluid in my own ears.

"What's the deal with the playdate later?" I ask the dad.

"No idea. Text our nanny with whatever you want to happen."

"Can it be at your house?"

"No. Please. Yours."

"I'll do it next time, I swear."

"I'm going to have Leo tell Penny about the existence of Legoland."

"You wouldn't dare."

"Oh yes. It's happening."

"Fuck me. Fine. My place."

He holds his hand up in the air, backing away, victorious, as we head to our separate subway platforms.

And then I'm off.

I go downtown in order to concentrate, in order to feel like myself again. I head to the Village, where I share an office with two other writers and one psychiatrist. Yup. Three writers and one psychiatrist to give us all the pills and comfort we need to sustain life as writers.

I put on headphones and listen to music as the train rattles beneath me.

This is when my day really begins. I'm lucky to have this arrangement. A coffee shop is too noisy and distracting. A library is too quiet. Can't bring coffee or eat a handful of cashews? Give me a break. *Librarians*. Put them in charge of the book fair.

I get to work. I sit down at my computer. I say to my brain: *Okay, it's time! Let's do it!* But then I end up spending a good portion of the morning opening invitations to children's birthday parties. *Let's Get Ready to Tumble!* Do we have to? *A spa birthday party for Sloane!* Oh good. My five-year-old has been dying for a detox.

These parties are brutal. Sometimes they try to make it fun for the parents. But a children's birthday party will never be fun for adults. Because there are children there. Occasionally, something amusing will happen, like the magician will ask the birthday boy what he wants to be when he grows up and he'll say, "A doorman!" And the parents will die of public humiliation and that'll be somewhat worth the price of admission.

As I mark my calendar, a bunch of texts come through on the parent group chain.

Why don't we start a letter-writing campaign, and the kids can write each other letters all summer?!

I LOVE this idea, Rebecca! How did you even think of it??

How *do* they come up with these things? Sometimes I'm

tempted, late at night, to start drunk texting the group: *You guys up?*

My phone dings again and again. I turn in the chair and then push away from the desk, flinging myself on wheels across the room. A text from the scooter dad: *It always feels like we're on a date. And it's going well.*

The man is smitten. I decide to play naive. *What? Seriously? Whatever do you mean?* But he calls my bluff. I say: *I know. I know. I just wanted to hear you elaborate.*

He smiles, I presume. No. I know. He's definitely smiling. He says: *I wish we were in some dark bar with finished drinks between us, feeling woozy.*

I write it all down. Keep texting. Squeeze the lemon for every drop. I start editing the conversation on the page, perfecting the dialogue, changing the situation. I put the words into the mouth of a character that starts off like him but ends up nothing like him at all. But I have nowhere to go with this. I throw my phone across the room.

Then I go back to it. I start calling my friends, pumping them for information.

"Is your divorce final yet?"

"Whatever happened to your brother-in-law . . . in the . . . hospital?"

"Remember that trip to Thailand . . . where you got food poisoning?"

I call my more rebellious friends, people I know from shows.

"What happened at that protest again?"

"Did they end up pressing charges?"

"And you were faking orgasms for this *entire* relationship?"

"All right," one says, finally. "I'll confess this to you. But don't put it in your book."

"Absolutely," I say, typing.

I can't help it. I will turn over everyone I know and shake every last penny out of their pockets.

Once I'm off the phone, I go for a walk around Washington Square Park, circling and circling, until I get hungry.

I stop on MacDougal Street at a place that makes "authentic Indian cart food." It is right next to a shop that specializes in oatmeal, and across from a store that sells exclusively popcorn. God, I love New York.

And then I return to my Word document and do important work like making sure that everything on my desk is symmetrical. Still nothing on the page.

It's two P.M. Time to get on the subway to pick my daughter up at school. My workday is over.

In the pickup line, I make a vow. *I am going to be patient. I am going to be kind. I am going to play Candy Land like I mean it.*

I am also listening, waiting, for somebody to say something interesting. But everyone is talking about the summer. They are discussing how hard it is to pack up a family of four for a European vacation. *It's no joke,* they say. I am not going to Europe, but the herd mentality is kicking in and I'm feeling the need to go to Europe. *Is it too late?*

One mom is going to Ibiza. Another is headed to Saint-Tropez. The moms with older children are giddy about sleepaway camp. They are counting the days until they can put their kids on the bus to Maine.

"And then I'll have twenty-seven days to myself before visiting day!"

Yup. Twenty-seven days of uninterrupted exercise classes, shopping, and cosmetic procedures! Botox from head to pinky toe.

The teacher opens the door. I take my daughter's snack out of my bag, with no small amount of trepidation. The snack must be transferred within two-point-three seconds of her leaving school. If I stumble, if I fall, there will be frustration. Yelling. Tears.

She emerges from the building.

The transfer is made.

"I want to sit on the couch and slouch," she says, as she walks down Park Avenue, hand in her fruit snacks.

"You mean lounge?"

"Oh. *Lounge.*"

A good sign. *Watch TV. Eat sugar. Shoot up. Just please let me get some work done.*

When we get home, I put on *The Lion King*, then *The Lion King 2*, then some TV show dedicated to *The Lion King* but with real lions. I sit in bed with my laptop on my stomach and try to come to grips with the fact that I haven't written anything all day—in months, to be clear. My agent keeps calling, and I silence the phone.

My son is with our nanny, building something with blocks, occasionally pulling down a lamp. My daughter comes into my bedroom every fifteen seconds to talk to me about a wide variety of topics, like bubblegum—how it works, how old you have to be to chew it.

"I can get you some," I say.

She shakes her head. "No. I'm not ready."

I make dinner. I give baths. I put them in pajamas. I read stories, vaguely paying attention to whatever is happening with the mouse and the giant strawberry. My husband comes home just in time to tuck them in, all clean and pajama-clad. The sweetest part of the day and he gets it. In my next life, I'm coming back as a dad.

My daughter jumps out of bed. "I can't stop thinking about lions," she says, and I drag her back. The baby cries. I sing to him.

How much is that doggie in the window? Arf-arf. I do hope that doggie's for sale. Arf-arf.

"He's still crying," I say to Alejandro. "Why is he *still* crying?"

"You're singing a song about adoption."

And then, they are asleep. The apartment is quiet. We are done. We lie on the couch and stare into space. Alejandro wants to watch a show about Vikings. I want to watch the Kardashians get their hair done in their oversized mansions. I should work. I'm finally free. But I can do nothing. I can only listen to the gentle hum of Kourtney's anxiety about how she's a control freak, they all are, and it's their mother's fault.

My agent calls again, and I let it ring. If necessary, I will pull a full-blown Costanza and hide under my desk. *My next book?* He'll have to find me first.

On Saturday night, I sneak out of the house at eleven to go to a concert. I don't really have to sneak, but if Alejandro hears me then he'll have free rein to leave me with the kids some other night and stay out as late as he wants, and I don't feel like giving him that ace in his pocket unless I get caught.

After the show, while I'm in a taxi home, crossing the Brooklyn Bridge, the phone rings from an unknown number. I watch it ring. *So late?* I'm tempted. I pick up.

"You're alive."

It's my agent.

"It's two in the morning!"

"You weren't answering my calls during business hours. I figured I had to pretend to be an ex-boyfriend calling with regrets in order to reach you."

"Well played."

"I'm calling because I have a client with an empty house in the Hamptons for the summer, in case you were interested in getting away from your family and getting some actual writing done, not that that's the kind of thing you'd be interested in."

"Which client?"

"Don't make me say it. You know which one."

"He said that I can use his house? *Why?*"

"You know he loves you."

"He loves all women."

"For lack of a better way of saying this . . . You're special."

"I feel sick, suddenly."

"Okay. I'll stop."

"Well, I can't leave my family for the entire summer! I'd be excommunicated from society. People would throw tomatoes at me whenever I left the house."

"What about . . . say . . . a month?"

I inhale dramatically. "Maybe . . . maybe . . . Would anyone else be there?"

"No. You'd be completely alone."

"Completely alone? What about a sexy gardener, or a nosy pool guy?"

"Nope."

"Neighborhood eccentric?"

"Completely alone."

"I don't know if I could handle that. I'm a city girl, with a family. I'm never alone. On a slow day, I have four doormen at my disposal."

"Think of it as an exercise in resilience. Alone and roughing it in the wilds of the Hamptons."

"*Will she survive?* Or will she finally learn about love, family, sex, greed, jealousy . . . life. Maybe she'll finally learn about the ties that bind them . . . Or will there be a devastating event that changes everything?"

"For a novelist, you have a surprising amount of hostility toward book jackets. Look. Maybe you'll get some material out of it. It'll build character. Maybe even a character or two."

"So, this house . . . Is it an adorable charming little shack with creaky floors and ghosts in the attic and maybe the electricity goes out sometimes and I'll have to write by candlelight?"

"It's the Hamptons. It's small, but unlikely haunted."

"Damn."

"I can have somebody go in and cut the electric sometimes if that's what it takes?"

"See, now you're really working for me, babe."

To take off from my family for a month, I know I have to do something drastic. And it has to involve tears. Alejandro knows I've been struggling, so this won't be shocking to him. He's been seeing my mental health deteriorate as the book deadline looms. But I have to pull out all the stops. So I pretend to be going insane, which I very nearly am. I believe, in the psychiatric business, it is called "leveling up."

When he gets home from work, I am high as a kite and organizing my books. I have taken all our books off the shelves and thrown them into the center of the room. I start reshelving them by size, color, author name, period in my life that I read them, you name it. I tell him I've been doing this all day.

"You didn't write today? When is your deadline again?" he asks.

And then I start to cry. I explain the situation. My agent and his evil demands that I comply with a contractual obligation. *That monster.*

I stare at him, maniacally, with glassy eyes. "I think I have to go to the Hamptons."

"*Really?*" he says, in a mocking tone. "This is the only way you can write?"

"I see no other way."

When I first get to the house, it's late at night and I am still not well, mentally. I spend all my time looking out the windows, searching for any sign of life. But I'm surrounded by farmland. It is a degree of black I am unused to. Across the farm, I can see a light or two, in the great distance, perhaps the home of the farmer who owns the land. But it is so far away that it is barely discernable from the reflections inside my house. There are a few houses around me, but I can't see them because of shrubbery or patches of woods. There is only one house, much larger than mine, that lurks close by. It is so large that it looms over the row of trees and hedges that separates our houses on one side. The windows are dark.

I can hear cars whizzing by sometimes, but there is not a person in sight. In the city, I like to sit at my window to see other human beings, potentially overhear their conversations. In this house, I see and hear nobody. On my first night, I make a lot of calls to Alejandro. I fall asleep at three A.M. to the sound of my fourth *Friends* episode. I don't get any writing done the next day because I'm disoriented. Also, *super* busy on neighborhood watch.

On my second night, I hear a car on gravel. I jump. *Finally*. I see the shine of headlights against my window, followed by the rumble of feet and the sound of voices next door. *Voices!* I run to the window, like a golden retriever desperate for its owner.

There is a lit window. *A lit window!* Just a yellow square, but it is the sweetest sight. It calms something inside me. Gives me a profound sense of well-being. The light is all I need. I sit down at my computer and imagine people milling about the house, and it is infinitely comforting to me. I go back to the window, staring at the light, making sure it hasn't disappeared. Then, I go about my business. But I keep coming back.

I write. I check for the light. I read. I check for the light. As long as it's on, I am okay. I am among friends. It has been only two hours and yet I fear the light being taken away from me. Before I go to sleep, I keep the shades only halfway down. Watching television in bed, I feel I have company, like I'm watching with somebody I know in the next room. I lower the shade just enough that I can still see the light as I drift off to sleep.

The next morning, I awaken to what sounds like a hundred people in a backyard. I never heard cars. Or anyone coming or going. Just the sudden sound of a hundred people. *How did they get there? Are the cars parked on the other side of the house? Was there . . . a party bus?* I can't figure it out. I sit outside by the pool, consumed by voices. I write their words down for a college party scene I'm working on, a play on the ancient Greek tradition of symposium. Basically—a drinking party. It must be a "darty," or daytime party. I've heard my sixteen-year-old babysitter throw around this term.

I listen to the partygoers on the other side of the bushes. How old are these people? I try to figure it out.

A thumping bass. Mass confusion. A crescendo of screams and squeals. Somebody yelling, *Alex!* An Alex is needed. *Do you need any help?* A humanitarian in the crowd. *Hey Ava! Let's do it.* A jumble of *What's up?* And: *What the fuck! Ava. Chill. AVA. Amaaaazing.* The sound of banging on the wall of a porta-potty. *Hey man, do you have a . . . Awwww don't think like that. WHAT? AHHH! WOO!* More banging. *I gotta piss, bro! Hi Sara . . . I miss you! Olympia, STOP!*

Conclusion: It's a bunch of young people of indeterminate age having a party. At ten A.M. Well, I can live with that. Brings a little life to the neighborhood.

I make myself a watermelon margarita. I have to write a sex scene now and I could use some loosening up. I down half my drink, then go for a swim. I spend the next five days alternating between writing, swimming, and spying on the house next door.

In just a week, my body has gone from a little bit soft to tan and taut. There's something about the water that is particularly conducive to my creativity. I write for a sprint and then go for a swim, let the ideas space out in my brain, and then I come out of the water, refreshed and energized and so eager to jot everything down that I'm typing while still dripping in my towel. I take off my bathing suit and admire my tan lines, walk around the top floor of the house naked. It's something I've never done before, but I've gotten into it. The tan lines make me feel like I'm wearing clothes.

I take a shower, put clothes back on, and write. I look out the window, examining the top floor of the other house. There is a little balcony where I always see girls, three or four of them, sitting and chatting, sometimes just one talking on the phone. But today there is a guy there with one girl and they are naked. I gasp and fall to the ground. The nakedness is shocking. *In broad daylight!* They start to kiss, and I watch as they continue to kiss, and then have sex, on this balcony, right before my eyes. I start laughing. I have to call someone. *But who would care about this?* This is amazing. I look away. *Who am I kidding?* I keep watching.

Ten minutes later, I still can't stop. They are young and their bodies are perfect, with tan lines of their own. I try to figure out this couple. Is this their first hookup or have they done this before? I think: I should be writing this down. But what would I even write? I'm intrigued, mildly jealous. I think about calling Alejandro, but what would that really do for me? The eagerness of these two.

I become obsessed with what is going on at that house. How many people live there? I strain to try to overhear the guys, the girls on the balcony, the conversation in the driveway. *What do they do each day?* I study the pattern of lights in the house. The main lights seem to be on past midnight every night. One of the bedrooms has its light on until four in the morning. Cars pull in after eleven all the time, the headlights crossing my window and bed, then the sound of their feet crunching on gravel, chatter about the night they've just had.

One night, the bass of their music startles me awake. It doesn't sound like a raging party. It sounds like a fucking earthquake.

I get so fed up that I put on jean shorts and a T-shirt and stomp over there, in the dark, using the flashlight on my phone as I walk through the woods.

I walk past three No Trespassing signs up to the house. This time the steps I hear against the gravel are mine. In the driveway, there are two crappy cars, old and beaten up, and one shiny black Ferrari.

I ring the bell. No answer. I knock on the door. No answer. I look through the opaque glass window on the door and can't see anyone inside. I turn the knob. It's open. I go in.

There is a pair of Vans near the door. The house is neat, a typical Hamptons rental, with white linen–covered couches and white oversized chairs, blue lamps, rustic wood tables, and bowls of shells everywhere. I keep walking. It is all very orderly, but for the kitchen table, which is covered in circular tins of chewing tobacco, at least three Ziploc bags filled with weed, and cartons of energy bars. A vase filled with flowers sits in the center of the table. Next to the flowers, there is a pitcher of water, ice, and cucumber slices, and next to that, a gun.

Are these people taking care of their bodies, or destroying them? The evidence is conflicting.

I hold my breath. I am tempted to back out, to run away, but I'd like to sleep tonight, and they probably wouldn't shoot a girl. I'm too cute. Too cute to shoot.

I keep walking, more cautiously now. I continue to follow the music, my ears ringing from the onslaught of sound, and open the screen door to the backyard. Outside, there is one guy. *One guy?*

I can't believe it. Not a party. Not hundreds of people. Just one guy, standing in flip-flops, shirtless, with the gray trim of his boxers sticking out at the waistband of his black mesh shorts. He is shooting hockey pucks on what appears to be a large square of synthetic ice, firing off pucks at a goal in the distance, while smoking a joint. He seems out of his mind, but he's also hitting every single target. *Is he experiencing some kind of psychotic episode?*

"HELLO?" I yell, staring at the back of his head, which is unmoving. He is staring at the goal.

He doesn't respond. He doesn't even turn, just keeps taking shots and drags from his joint. I shout a little louder: "EXCUSE ME? EXCUSE ME? HELLO?"

He turns, and he is so blindingly good-looking that my first thought is not about his body, the every single muscle that you can see as he shoots, the blondish-brown hair sticking out of the navy bandana that he's got wrapped around his head, or even the textbook face. My first thought is: *He must not be in possession of two brain cells to rub together.*

He stares at me, as if I'm the one who needs to explain myself.

"THE MUSIC?" I yell. "IT'S A LITTLE LOUD."

He takes another drag from his joint and goes back to firing. I stomp over to a speaker and spend about five seconds looking for a knob before kicking it over with my foot, then unplugging it.

"Are you fucking kidding me?" he says.

"Are *you*?" I demand, hands on hips.

"Who the fuck are you?"

"Your neighbor. Your very *disturbed* neighbor who doesn't think she should have to stay up all night just because you're listening to African techno music at a decibel level not suited for the human ear."

He laughs. "Not suited for the human ear, huh? Go back to the city . . . " He goes over to the speaker and plugs it back in, turns it on.

He is taking shots again. I stare at him, dumbfounded, and then turn to walk away.

"I'll tell you what," I hear him say, as I'm about to walk through the door. I stop. I turn.

He puts his joint down into a plastic cup. "If you can hit that goal, *once*, I'll turn the music off, and it'll be like a fucking library over here." He offers me his stick. He raises his chin in my direction, holding out the stick. As I stand there, frozen, he looks me up and down.

I walk over, step onto the white square, take the stick from his hands. He puts the puck down.

"You get one chance," he says.

"Five," I reply.

He laughs. "*Five?* Get out of here."

"Give me five or I call the police and report a noise violation. I'm sure they'd be *fascinated* by your kitchen table." I smile.

"Three," he says.

"Fine."

I take a shot, and the puck goes sailing to the left, into a pot of flowers that is about four feet from my side. He puts another puck down. I am focused. I am determined to stop the madness. I shoot and miss the puck altogether, then shoot again and it dribbles onto the grass. My third shot goes in the general direction of the goal but stops significantly short of it.

"Fuck," I say, and then throw the stick to the ground. He laughs and goes over to the music, turning it up even louder.

"*Asshole,*" I mutter under my breath and stomp toward the door.

"Come back and practice your shot again sometime!" he yells after me. "And welcome to the neighborhood!"

3

CARTER

I AM MAKING COFFEE WITH A coffee machine I didn't buy, in a kitchen I don't own. I stayed out later than everyone else last night, yet somehow I'm up first. Yup. It's just me and the girls, the random girls strewn about the house. They're in the bedrooms. They're by the pool. But they aren't making anybody breakfast, so that's what I do.

I pour raspberries and blueberries out of their green cartons onto a large plate. I cut peaches into neat slices. There's something soothing about this ritual, arranging fruit in the morning, like you can erase whatever chaos came the night before and start over.

I rent this house with my former college teammates, Harps and JT. Scott Harper is a goalie from upstate New York. He's quiet, so quiet that you can't tell if he's depressed or happy. You'd have to decipher whatever wildly outlandish thing he says under his breath. He's into astrological signs. From Monday to Thursday, he does sunrise yoga, reads the classics—Hemingway, Kerouac—and looks through his telescope. What's he looking at? Nobody knows. But then, Friday to Sunday, he goes, and he goes hard. Booze. Girls. A lot of cocaine.

Jack Thomas, JT, is a left winger from Canada. He loves electronic music, like deep house. He plays it every chance he gets. He dresses like a white rapper and doesn't give a fuck about anything. He's always high, always going up or down. He sniffs out all the late-night parties. But he knows who he is. He's accepted it. And I mean that. He has an arm tattoo that says *I am what I am.*

A scout from the Rangers came to see me at UNH during my freshman year and ended up drafting all three of us. I was a first-round pick, meant to finish my degree and go straight from college to the NHL. JT and Harps will go to Hartford to play in the American League for a few years before they get a chance at the show. The Hartford Wolfpack is the New York Rangers' minor league team in the AHL. It's where most draft picks go to play for a few years until they're ready for the NHL.

I'm putting the peach slices next to the berries in an orderly fashion. The girls occasionally walk by with their tight tank tops, high ponytails, and 90s sunglasses, the thin lenses barely covering their eyes. They look like snakes.

There is a knock on the door and the sound of somebody letting themselves in.

"*Hello?*" a female voice bellows from the front hallway. It's JT's older sister, Jill.

"Hi," I yell back. "The guys are still asleep."

She comes into the kitchen wearing a long, pink-and-white checkered caftan and pink clogs. She's the one who hooked the boys up with their summer job, a catering gig. They'll make a ton of money, she assured them. I have a signing bonus, so I didn't need the job. All I had to do was spend the summer in close proximity to New York City to be available for the team.

I ask, "What'd you get up to last night?"

She doesn't respond, just sighs audibly, and then goes banging on doors, barging into the bedrooms clapping her hands and clicking her clogs, waking the guys up.

"What is going on in here?" she shouts from the upstairs hallway. "It's almost ten! Why isn't anyone awake? You do realize that you have an *obligation*?"

"Could you *chill*?" I hear JT say to her. "It's an eleven o'clock party. We have, like, ten hours."

"*What?* The party is at eleven *a.m.*!"

"Eleven *a.m.*?"

"Yes! It starts in an hour."

"What kind of party . . . It's not at night?"

"Why would you just *assume* it's at night?"

"It said, 'Welcome to the jungle' on the invitation! In neon lights! I thought it was a Guns N' Roses–themed rager."

"Oh my god. It's a nine-year-old's birthday party. Jungle-themed."

I start cackling.

Jill comes up to me, grabs my chin, and says in a sing-songy voice: "If you don't stop laughing, we won't bring you back any cake."

I shake my chin loose and get back to my fruit. She is aghast at our kitchen, holding up an empty bottle of tequila and throwing beer cans into a garbage bag. JT is walking around in his white wifebeater, looking confused.

"Your uniforms are at the venue," she says to him. "Just put on anything."

Harps puts on a hooded sweatshirt, left arm first. Like all goalies, he's superstitious. Left shoe first, left arm first. Always.

Jill says: "Christ. You're going to be late for your first gig. I'm so glad I recommended you for a job at Celebrate. That was a very shrewd move of mine." They start moving at a faster pace.

"That's what the company is called?" I ask. "*Celebrate*?"

"Yeah . . . so?"

I throw my hands up into the air. "It has no cachet, no island flair!"

She rolls her eyes and looks at the couch, starts collecting all the handbags off it.

"All right, ladies! Show's over. Ubers, everyone! Back to Gurney's! Last Jitney is leaving the station!"

One girl pouts and shouts something at her in Russian, presumably curse words.

JT crushes Adderall with a credit card onto the kitchen table. He and Harps both snort. Nose to table.

I shake my head at them. "You should have taken your Adderall an hour ago! You know what this is? This is an American League mindset. No berries for you."

They ignore me completely. Harps grabs a bag of hamburger buns for the road. JT drinks water out of what appears to be a vase, leaves without shoes on, then comes back for them.

"Have you seen my shoes?"

"Get the fuck out of here! Your lack of motivation is contagious," I say, and then catch a glimpse of the cover of the book on my kitchen counter. *The Mindful Path: 9 Weeks to Emotional Clarity and Inner Calm.* I had to take an anger management class in college, a decree from the coaching staff. I keep the book around as a reminder, occasionally flipping through it.

I fight the urge to say more to them. If I stop talking and focus on my breath, I might achieve inner calm. Also, I won't have to open that damn book.

"What are you going to do while we're gone?" JT asks me. "Don't get bored and fuck shit up, okay?"

"What am I going to fuck up here at this house at ten in the morning?"

JT throws his hands into the air. "Who knows what you're capable of?"

Jill holds the front door open, glares at JT. "He's fine! Let's go!"

JT yells back at her, "You think he's fine, and then suddenly some girl is calling me crying and he needs bail money! He's a stealth bomber!"

The entire crew funnels out, and suddenly I am alone in this house and it feels strange. When you're used to a steady level of noise, the quiet is jarring. But it feels good. I can lie around. Do whatever. Crank the music up.

I decide to go for a run.

It's a foggy morning. The windows are so clouded up that I can't see out of them. I open the door to get a sense of the day. The sky is white with a layer of mist transforming the landscape from green to gray. The further away the trees, the whiter they appear. Our house is mostly surrounded by woods. It is silent. I see a bird on one of the steps that leads up to our door. It is darting its head around, evaluating the situation, just like I am. I feel a certain camaraderie with this bird. I listen to it squawk, then wait with it in the silence for another to respond. I start to wonder about birds and if they're communicating with specific other birds or if every squawk is just a general message, out into the ether. *Is anybody out there?*

I hold my hand out to check for rain. If it's raining, I can sit inside and do nothing, which would be super. But it's not. I should go.

I go back inside, down a handful of berries, and then lace up my sneakers. I head down the street, running at a steady pace. I pass a few houses, their gardeners hard at work, trimming and raking. I wind up in front of a farm. I see a woman in black bike shorts and a black T-shirt, hair in a low ponytail, running toward me. Nice body. Is that the chick from a few nights ago? Looks different in a ponytail. She sees me and quickly darts to the opposite side of the road, passes me by.

Well, we can't have that.

"Hey!" I call, and then wait for a car to pass. I run across the street to catch up to her. She glances back and then stops running, stands there catching her breath. She has a look on her face that is not pleased.

I smile. "Did you finally get to sleep the other night?"

She rolls her eyes. "I did. Your evil plan didn't work."

"Huh?"

"Your evil plan . . . to keep me up all night."

"What?"

"*Huh? What?*" she says, mimicking me. "Clearly, your hearing is impaired. You should try turning the music down."

I laugh. "You know that expression . . . the music is so loud you can't hear yourself think? I believe that was the point . . . Anyway, um . . . Feel like we got off on the wrong foot." I stick my hand out. "Carter."

She looks at my hand, then shakes it.

"Jessica," she says, her slightly sweaty palm attached to mine.

On one side of us is an endless field of wheat, blowing in the breeze. On the other side, cars and trucks zoom by.

"Out for a run?" I ask her.

She smiles. "Nothing gets by you."

I look down. I like her sneakers. Or maybe it's her ankles.

I squint at her, holding my hand above my eyes to block the sun. "Do you want to race until the end of this wheat field?"

"I do not," she says, without hesitation.

"Why not? It'll be fun . . . or one of us will get hit by a Jeep Wrangler. Either way it'll be memorable."

Her eyes widen, suddenly animated. "Do you think it'd be a hit-and-run or would they hide the body?"

"Hide the body? Nobody in the Hamptons knows how to shovel."

She laughs, shakes her head.

"So, how about it? End of the field?"

"Absolutely not. I never run that way."

"Never? How come?"

"Because I don't have a *death wish*."

I laugh. "A death wish?"

"It's dangerous! The cars barely have room to avoid hitting each other, let alone swerving to avoid runners."

I look at the road. Looks safe to me.

"I don't even like to drive on this road," she says. "But I'm a lousy driver . . . I'm using the car of the guy whose house I'm borrowing and the other day, I accidentally drove it into town with the emergency brake on." She winces. "Also, I don't make left turns."

"What do you mean? Ever?"

"Nope. No thanks. Don't make 'em. Not interested."

"How do you get anywhere?"

She smiles. "I don't get very far, to be honest. But I've committed to a life without left turns. Some people don't eat meat. I don't make left turns."

"Thank god you ran into me," I say. "I'm gonna solve all your problems right now."

She puts her hands on her hips. "Oh really?"

"Hand signals."

She looks at me skeptically. "Hand signals?"

"You roll down your window and stick out your hand and make a big fuss to everyone involved over what move you're about to make. Honk your horn. Wave your hand up and down. Do whatever you have to do to get everyone's attention, then you can go wherever the fuck you want."

She laughs. "I'm not doing that."

"How about that race? Come on. Loser buys the winner lunch. I don't want to sweeten the deal too much, but I have a live lobster clawing its way around my house right now. You can put it in the pot yourself. I mean it—I'll just watch. You can do the honors."

She exclaims: "What if I were an animal rights activist?"

I laugh. "Are you?"

I feel like she can't fool me, like we've known each other for a while. This is Jessica. And Jessica is not an animal rights activist.

She points at me, smiles. "No . . . but you didn't know that." *Didn't I?*

She turns to run in the opposite direction. And then, suddenly, I'm desperate to keep her from leaving, this girl I barely know. I have the odd sensation that I'll miss her company. She's made me laugh three times in the past three minutes.

"I'll give you a five-second head start! Have you ever dropped a living thing in boiling water? It's *thrilling*."

She waves. "Bye, Carter."

When I get back from my run, I text the guys:

Going to the rink today. Pick you up in front of the party at 2.

I don't give them the option to weigh in, or to bow out.

I pick them up in my car after they're done with work and drive us all to the nearest rink, which is an hour away in Hauppauge. The manager of the rink made some kind of arrangement with the Rangers' strength and conditioning coach and the ice is available to us for the summer months, from six to eight A.M. or three to six P.M.

The drive takes us out of the unique area that is the Hamptons and into more standard suburbia. Here, in vague parts of Long Island that nobody talks about, it reminds me of where I'm from in Pennsylvania: a ramshackle town that has a tavern and a few memorials and not much else. It's kind of like going back in time. Johnstown, Pennsylvania: home of the steel plant where they invented barbed wire.

Ninety percent of the people I grew up with stayed there, became pipe fitters or electricians or worked in a mine, which I can almost guarantee you is not as much fun as it sounds. Iron, coal, or steel—take your pick. If someone is athletically gifted, they might make it out, but it doesn't happen too often. All my friends were basically fuckups. But my parents were teachers. The picture of middle-class stability. They weren't drug addicts or drunks, just people hardened from growing up in Johnstown, where there are a lot of floods, widows, death. The average annual household income is twenty-three thousand dollars, and twenty-six percent of families live below the poverty line. That I would someday require ice time within driving distance of the Hamptons was about as good a bet as the Americans beating the Russians in the 1980 Olympics.

When we get to the rink, everyone makes a big deal out of me being there. We shake hands with the manager, Tim McDonald. Tim has given us the referee's dressing room to leave our equipment in for the summer, so we don't have to lug it back and forth from the house.

JT takes a burning-hot shower before going out onto the ice, to warm himself up. Harps bounces a squash ball against the wall to get his auditory system going. He's quiet as he gets dressed, but fast. An NHL player should be able to go from undressed to dressed in under four minutes.

I'm all too familiar with their routines. They're not only my closest friends but also my training partners. It's our first summer in the Hamptons, but our fourth summer training together.

We walk out onto the ice. An arena has a different smell when it's hot outside. It's the lingering scent of work versus fun. Players on the ice during the summer are all business.

People start to gather around the rink to watch us. They take pictures.

The rink is a little watery. I tell Tim the setting on the Zamboni must be off. You need to use less water during the summer, because it's not as cold outside. He tells me he'll have that adjusted right away. The guys look at me like I'm nuts, but everything counts, and I'm not practicing on a watery rink while my competitors, in some other town, on some other practice rink, are getting it right.

As I circle the ice, JT starts chirping at me: "Ladies and gentlemen, the future holder of the record for most penalty minutes by a rookie in the NHL!"

Harps is laughing through his helmet.

"Can we get some music?" I say to Tim, who is standing at the side of the rink, watching us.

He shakes his head. "Sorry. House rule. No music during ice rentals."

I look at him with wide eyes. "Are you serious?"

JT turns to Harps and sighs. "Here we go."

Tim replies: "I'm afraid I can't break this particular rule. Not even for you, Hughes."

"I'm not asking you to break this rule. I'm asking you to invest in the future of the city of New York."

Tim laughs.

"We'll play better with music, don't you think? Don't you want us to go harder?"

He rolls his eyes.

I go on. "And what's the harm? You go for a run and wear your headphones, don't you? No music? Who made this rule? I guess I just really gotta question your dedication here, McDonald. Do you want to see the Rangers win a Stanley Cup or not?"

"Hughes . . . " Tim is caving.

I smile widely. "You're a team player, McDonald! I can feel it!"

Tim shakes his head and holds up his hands, laughs as he walks away. "I didn't see anything."

I skate over to the scorekeeper's box and plug my phone into the speaker system. I put on CMG The Label's album *Gangsta Art*.

We get Harps warmed up first. Two hundred shots in ten minutes. It's a feeding system whereby we shoot fifty pucks at his glove hand, fifty off his blocker, fifty right pad, fifty left pad. We play a game of one-on-one. Me versus JT. It gets the blood flowing. Our hands warmed up. The only rule is that there's no hooking or slashing because the last thing we need is a fight before we've even started the workout.

But then JT hits Harps on the shoulder with a shot and I go into defender move.

"You gotta keep your shot down in warmup! NHL players know how to control their shot!"

And then JT says: "Fuck you! I'm warming up too!"

We almost go at it, but don't. Hockey players have the unique ability to fight each other in any situation. Doesn't matter if they're brothers or best friends. Immediately after it's done, there's no grudge held. The fight is the removal of the grudge.

We have a forty-minute skill session. We work on stick handling, passing, careful to keep our heads up the entire time. We do one-on-one battle drills from below the hash marks. Transition into some shooting from the face-off dots. We practice quick-release shots. JT is giving me bad passes intentionally. I have a fraction of a second to adjust. There's no perfect pass in a game. And we want to practice like we play, to expect the unexpected.

It's a hundred shots from each corner. Harps has taken about a thousand shots at this point. By the end of forty minutes, it's up to three thousand.

I face off against JT in the offensive zone. We race and battle for the puck. JT is continually hooking me and I'm getting annoyed. After the sixth hook, I make a quick stop, turn, and slash JT with a two-handed baseball swing across his legs that snaps my stick in two.

He yells over at Harps, "Discipline's always been a problem with our buddy Carter."

I get in his face. "My hands are too expensive to fight you, but I get my sticks for free."

He shakes his head, skates away. "You're an arrogant piece of shit."

"Yeah, I am. You should try it sometime. You might make the team!"

He needs the motivation. To have my words ringing in his ears. That'll help him a lot more than if I told him a bedtime story.

We do a "bag skate" at the end, which is slang for when a coach gets angry, and they say: "We're gonna skate your bag off." We go from one end of the rink to the other, touching each line, then skating back to the original starting point.

When we finish, JT and Harps are keeled over. Dead. Ready to get off the ice.

"Let's have a breakaway competition," I say. "Five breakaways each. And then we can go home."

JT looks up at me. "You're serious?"

"If you don't have the ability to be the last man out and the first man on, you might as well just go the fuck home right now."

He stares at me, raises his arm toward the net. "Let's go."

The two of us square off against Harps for the next ten minutes. Then we tap our sticks on the ice and head off.

"How was the practice session, boys?" Tim says to us as we change back into our normal clothes.

"Oh, it was *awesome*," I reply. "Really great. Top level. Quite a facility you're running here, McDonald. Thank you very much for everything."

I am feeling fantastic. Take all the breaths you want. The only thing that never fails to manage anger? Physical exhaustion.

"He's getting all the bounces today," JT says, glancing back at me. "Picking all the corners. He got his music. We can all rest easy now."

"The only rest you need is a nap this afternoon so that you're ready to go tonight," I say.

Tim laughs. "I guess I won't be seeing you guys in the morning."

"You'll see me," I say.

4

JESSICA

I SEND AN EMAIL TO MY agent: *100 pages down!!!!!!* He hates exclamation marks, but I use them anyway. You can't tell me when to exclaim.

To reward myself, I lie in the sun on a lounge chair and think about sex. Not directly and not all the time. It's more like a train that runs by once or twice an hour. The sun has dimmed my brain and made my skin feel prickly, extra sensitive. Plus I'm reading this Miranda July book, and even though it's mildly depressing (the woman in the book has an affair with a guy who works at a Hertz rent-a-car), she's pretty into it, the narrator, so I take the day off to transport myself, via July, to what's happening in a seedy motel room off the side of a highway in California.

I always celebrate when I hit this mark. So this time, I'm celebrating by lying around, doing nothing, and getting hit with a few seconds of bliss on a rolling basis. Who is to say what constitutes a celebration?

Of course, I'm also thinking about how Miranda July has written three movies, two collections of short stories, and two novels. I need to get cracking. Eventually. But July is fifty years old. I am thirty-five. A young thirty-five. We have nothing in common.

I am spending most of my time outside, writing on my covered porch, laptop sitting on my bare legs, the heat from the computer burning the tops of my thighs. Sometimes I drive into town for a sandwich or to immerse myself in the outside world, but I don't do that very often, for fear of encountering a parallel parking situation.

At night, I sit on the steps of my house and look at the fireflies, watch as the specks of yellow spark and then disappear into the growing blackness. Aside from the occasional bout of guilt that I swat away like a mosquito, it is a pleasant experience.

Page one hundred and one is looming, but I've hit a wall. I don't know what to say next. It's easy to set up, to fling your characters into the air, but not so easy to make the acrobatics happen once they get there.

I sit with my laptop and stare into space. I have nothing. I go into the kitchen and make myself a watermelon margarita, grab my phone from the kitchen table. I go back outside, lie down on my stomach, untie the top of my bathing suit. *Who's here to see me?* If anyone asks, I am simply taking a break from writing. I am hard at work on my tan lines.

I call Alejandro and we give each other polite recaps.

He tells me that our daughter lost a tooth, but he accidentally threw it out. I tell him about the hundred pages, the swimming, the fireflies.

"You are really living it up there," he says, and I can't argue. Because no matter what I'm doing, he's the one searching the garbage for a tooth.

"I'll call you tonight," I say. "You'll be home, right?" He says he has a work dinner, but after that, yes.

I haven't been alone like this for fifteen years. It's peaceful and easy in a way, to only be obliged to take care of yourself, but I also feel the missing piece, always. I feel like a body without an arm, searching for something to make me whole but having no idea where to find it. *I am a whole person,* I tell myself. *The rest of you is just two hours away, give or take traffic.* But I make a lot of calls. I keep people on the phone longer than I should. I make conversation with the UPS man, the Amazon guy. I feel relief when the van arrives with my Fresh Direct, and I have an amusing back-and-forth with the driver. I think: *Maybe this is something?*

I am not supposed to be searching for something outside myself. But I am searching for something outside myself. Aside from the luxury SUVs speeding by, my neighbors are the only source of life around me, and thank god. It's come in handy. I am writing a book about a group of twentysomethings, and occasionally I'll hear the chatter of the girls or bros filtering in and out of their house, and I get something that I can include in my novel. *Finally,* I think, *something I can use.*

There is one guy who is always predicting the weather:

"It's about to rain. I can feel it in my bones. I feel more elastic the past few days."

There is talk of produce each time they return from the farmstand:

"*These fucking berries. Twenty-two dollars for strawberries. Harry's berries. Who is Harry anyway?*"

"*He'd better be the fucking head of the Department of Agriculture at these prices.*"

I laugh. Jot it down. There is a lot about working out:

"*I saw on TikTok that Cialis is actually considered the best pre-workout on the market.*"

"*Holy shit! It makes sense though. It's a stimulant. Adderall without the methamphetamine. It gets your blood flowing.*"

"*Dude, that hot yoga class? The room wasn't nearly hot enough. Turn the fucking heat up! They got it at 108. Should be 120. I don't want to do yoga with a bunch of pussies!*"

"*Who did you think was going to be in a hot yoga class in the Hamptons? It's rich moms.*"

There is commentary on the relative hotness of the girls in town:

"*What about the girl who works at Cynthia Rowley? Is she on Instagram? Do you think she's dirty? She looks like she's dirty.*"

"*She wears an anklet. I love a girl with an anklet.*"

"*Ah, yeah. Me too. Anklets are hot.*"

I make an amazed look at nobody. Sometimes I'll hide near the hedges so that I can hear better. But I don't have to do that often. Most of the time, they're yelling.

Today, two of them are playing some game on their front lawn. It sounds like a cross between tennis and wrestling. I hear the smack of a ball being hit, along with a lot of grunting and sweaty bodies slapping against each other.

And then I hear shouting, followed by the distinct sound of two people falling through my hedges.

I prop myself up on my forearms, then, realizing that I'm basically topless, rush to tie my bathing suit behind my neck. I watch them as they get off the ground, dust themselves off.

"Wow. Sorry!" one says to me. The other is lying on the ground, examining his wounds. "Didn't mean to startle you."

I laugh. "I'm startled. Are you okay?"

The top halves of their shirtless bodies are all scratched up.

"Can I get you a Band-Aid or something?" I get up from the lounge chair. "I'm sure I have Band-Aids . . . somewhere."

"What's a Band-Aid?" one says. "I haven't put a Band-Aid on since I was eight. You gotta let the cut breathe, babe." He points at me, with a look of warning.

I smile. "Okay, well then I have nothing to offer you."

They look me over. "Are you sure? You got any iced tea?"

I look down, thinking. "No, but I do have watermelon margaritas!" I raise my eyebrows at them, hopeful.

"Sold!" one says. The other nods silently.

I am thrilled. *Company*! I rush to the kitchen. I go inside and open the fridge, take out my pitcher.

"I'm Jack," the taller, louder guy says. "This is Scott." Scott doesn't say much. Jack is his representative.

I pour them two glasses. "So what are you guys up to over there? I can't tell. Is it . . . football?"

"Spike ball."

"Spike ball?"

"Fastest growing sport in America."

"Okay. What is it?"

"It's a game where we hit a ball at a net with our hand and try to kill each other."

"Sounds civilized."

"What do you do?"

"I'm a writer."

"I used to date a girl that wrote about beauty products for Instagram. Well, she mostly talked about them. But she wrote her own captions . . . I think."

I smile. "I write books."

"You'd better watch out for that AI," Jack says. He is, again, pointing at me.

I laugh. "Great tip. Thank you. I will."

He goes on: "Scott here is a big reader. He has the entire Hemingway collection in his room. He's reading one right now. Which one are you reading again, Harps?"

"*To Have and Have Not*," Scott replies.

I wince. "Personally, I think Hemingway is a little overrated."

They are stunned silent.

Suddenly, it occurs to me that I now have a direct line. I can ask them anything. They won't say no. They're holding my glasses.

"Actually . . . While you're here, do you mind if I ask you some questions? I'm writing a book that involves people around your age. I could use some intel."

Jack lies down on a lounge chair. "Fire away."

"Tell me about a typical night out in college these days," I say, and they launch into some stories.

I ask: "And what if you meet a girl you like? Are you texting her right after, the next day, or what?"

They tell me how Instagram has taken over, that nobody gets a girl's phone number anymore. Texting is obsolete. It's all about the DM.

I say, "But it must be strange to look somebody up on Instagram, to know all these details about their life before you actually get to know them? And you haven't even gotten to know 'them,' per se. You're just familiarizing yourself with their online persona."

"But that's key!" Jack insists. "That's how they want the world to see them!"

"It's tricky, though . . . " I say. "Because then you have to separate their exterior versus interior life. You have to figure out what specifically is broken inside of them that is causing them to post this or that. You have to ask yourself: Who is this for? What message are they pushing? In my day, that was harder to figure out. You had to go on at least three dates before you knew what was deeply wrong with a person."

They give me a dazed look. Jack says, "I just want enough information so that I can enter the zone cleanly."

I laugh. "Okay. Last question. For now. Why is there only one expensive car in your driveway?"

"That's Carter's. He's drafted and signed, whereas we're just drafted."

I'm tempted to ask them more about Carter, but I don't.

"Tell us about your glory days," Jack says. "I bet you were all sorts of trouble."

"No. No. Nothing crazy. I never really liked rebellion for the sake of rebellion. But I liked to try things, to explore, to test the limits . . . I was always a bit of a flight risk, had a flair for the dramatic, wasn't so interested in being tied down . . ."

The quiet one speaks up. "And now?"

"I'm married with children, so I'm certainly tied down." I smile. "The problem with marriage . . . Well, one of the many problems, is that it doesn't change your entire personality. And I'm sort of a restless person by nature."

He nods knowingly, though I'm sure he doesn't know.

They finish their drinks. They seem completely unaffected by the alcohol content. I can't relate. One drink and I'll tell you anything.

"Well, it's been nice chatting," I say.

"Yeah!" They put their glasses down on the table. "Thanks for the refreshments. Hey. Tonight. Game seven of the Stanley Cup finals. We're going to watch the game and have a little party. You should come! See some actual twentysomethings in the wild . . . " Jack is grinning widely.

"Oh, I don't know," I say. "I'm not much of a hockey fan."

"Starts at seven. Come one, come all."

"I don't think so, but . . . " I shrug. "I may change my mind."

"All right."

"To go or go not," I say to the Hemingway fan. He bows his head at me.

As they turn to leave, I stare at their bodies. These are some fit men. Greek god–like. Nobody in the neighborhood looks like this. These are physical specimens. Everywhere they go, they must stand out. Hence the girls. It must be so easy to get laid.

Once they've left, back through the hedges, I jot down some notes. I might have gotten a few pages out of it. Worth the damage to the shrubs. Especially since the shrubs aren't mine.

I have a long night of nothing ahead of me. I go for a walk, watch TV, read, but I am itching for something more, desperate to go out and interact with other humans. I call a few friends who are in the area, but they're all with their kids, in the middle of bath time or putting them to sleep. Alejandro is on his seventh course at Milos, a Greek restaurant in midtown that serves some special kind of branzino that only investment bankers can afford.

I try to go to bed early, but I can't sleep. I listen to the music next door.

Should I go to the party? I get a laugh out of that idea. *What would I even do there?*

I go outside, sit on the steps to my house, and stare at the rustling trees, the moon, the cars on the street turning into the house next door. Cars begin to park along the road in front of my house, their headlights illuminating my driveway, followed by voices in the distance.

Tonight, I can handle. But then I think about tomorrow. Page one hundred and one staring back at me. The cursor blinking on the blank page. You know what? Maybe I just need something to happen. Life has been stagnant lately. Maybe I need a little turmoil. And since when am I a stranger to that? I sneak out of my own apartment on a regular basis, for crying out loud. Talking to the guys about my twenties reminds me of who I am now, at my core, which is less trouble, but still some.

I'll just walk over there. I can always turn back.

I go back upstairs to the bedroom, fix my hair in the bathroom mirror. I put on a white short-sleeved terry cloth dress that hugs my body, and a layer of lip balm. I go downstairs, scour the liquor cabinet for something that won't be missed. There are only half-empty bottles of gin and tequila. I open the wine fridge and consider a bottle of wine. *Do these guys drink wine? Am I supposed to be pilfering the liquor at this place?* A lot of unanswered questions. I march down my driveway into the hot night with a bottle in hand.

In search of material. I am nothing if not a dedicated professional.

I turn onto their driveway, past the procession of PRIVATE ROAD and NO TRESPASSING signs. I am moving my hips to avoid the side mirrors of parked cars. It is tricky, with every mirror caught in a muddle of branches from the trees beside the driveway. It would be easier to get to the house if I walked through the woods surrounding the driveway, but I can't do that. I am by no means an outdoorswoman, but a short white dress and flip-flops do not strike me as woods attire.

Once I'm closer to the house, I see that there is a gigantic flat-screen television, with the game on, and people yelling around it. It smells like burgers and hot dogs. There is a crowd of bodies in every room. The music is thumping.

I think: *All right. Time to turn back.* I don't belong here. I should go home, before somebody throws up on me. I should just enjoy the lit windows and not being completely alone here in the woods. Isn't that the ideal situation, to be alone but have the low rumble of a party going on in the distance that you don't have to attend? I turn to leave.

But then I look up at the moon, and it's like the moon is teasing me. Another night of moon staring, huh? No. I have immersed myself in nature. I have watched sunsets, smelled flowers, listened to the wind. No. I have stared at the moon for long enough. The moon and I are *over*.

"I love your dress," a girl says to me, passing by, as I stand there frozen in the driveway. "Thanks," I reply, looking down. I slip inside the house.

5

CARTER

WE'RE DONE TRAINING FOR THE DAY. Game seven of the Stanley Cup Finals is on. I have a house full of a hundred of my closest acquaintances. What more could you want from a summer night in the Hamptons? I am flying high, *high,* as I move about the living room full of girls trying everything in the book to get me to go up to my bedroom.

Can I do cocaine in your bathroom?
Sure. Go ahead.
You won't do a bump with me?
Maybe later.
I'm cold. Do you have a sweatshirt I can borrow?
You can check.

I don't go. I don't go because it's too *easy.* I've seen this dance before. It's sex without the chase. Hard pass.

Then I see my neighbor walk into our house in a white dress, like a fucking angel. She looks so sophisticated and cool, like she should be at a different party. And yet: *What's she doing here?* Maybe I wasn't so repulsive to her, after all.

"Decided to join in on the action, huh?" I say, approaching her.

She replies: "I'm not technically crashing. Your friends invited me."

"They did?"

"Well, first they fell through my hedges. Then they invited me."

I look across the room, at JT and Harps sitting on our couch and watching the game. I am suddenly overcome with affection for them. "You gotta love 'em."

My hand instinctively moves to touch her bare forearm, but I pull it quickly away, as if touching something hot.

"Let me get you a drink."

She doesn't reply. I turn to go. I turn back. "Is beer okay?"

She shrugs. "Sure."

There is a goal called off. It's going to a review. Everyone is yelling.

"Bullshit. There's no way that's offside," I hear JT say.

I reply, "They changed the rule. If a player's skate is in the air but isn't completely in the offensive zone, he's onside."

"I guess I didn't get the memo."

I shake my head. "There's that American League mindset again."

"Fuck off."

I go to the kitchen and return to Jessica with her beer. "So what's all this about you playing for the Rangers?" she asks. "Madison Square Garden. Center of the universe."

"Have you been to a game?"

She looks up, thinking. "No, but I've gone to many concerts there. My first was Bob Dylan when I was ten. Who else? Eric Clapton, Billy Joel, Elton John. Um . . . Phish, Grateful Dead, Dave Matthews, of course. You're going to have to put on quite a show."

"I'm planning on it."

"You sound sure of yourself."

"No other way to be."

She nods, takes a long sip and then squints across the room, through the windows, at the table on our patio, which is littered with red cups. "Is that beer pong?"

"It sure is."

She takes another sip. "Can I play?"

I glance outside. "You want to play beer pong?"

"Yes," she says. "I sure do."

I laugh and motion for her to lead the way.

We wait beside the table for the current game to finish. Jessica sips her beer. When the new game begins, I make sure we are teammates.

I miss my first shot but then sink the next two. She sinks her first two.

"I don't want this to go to your head, but . . ."

"I know," she says. "I'm very good."

"Ah. So it's already gone to your head."

She laughs, clutching her beer. Before long, we are within

certain victory. With three cups left, she sinks two. I hit the last one. A new set of opponents wants to play. They begin setting up the cups.

"I see now why you wanted to play," I say.

"I play to win," she replies, swaying around, ignoring me in favor of the music.

She's not kidding. She is hyperfocused on winning. She turns to the table. "Can you make the triangle a little tighter?" she says to the other team, arranging our cups.

Soon she's all fired up about one guy who keeps leaning over the table. "His wrist is halfway across the table! An inch further and he'll be touching my stomach!"

Instinctively, I look down. Her dress is tight around her hips, and I can see the faint outline of her body.

"What do you want me to do about it?" I ask. "Lock him in the basement? Call a violation!"

"I'm not calling a violation! That's absurd."

At one point, our opponent sneezes. "Bless you," I say.

Jessica turns to me. "*Why would you say that?* He's our enemy."

"It was a hesitant 'bless you.' My heart wasn't in it."

"He's our enemy *and* he's cheating."

"Don't have such a chip on your shoulder."

"I always play with a chip on my shoulder. That's why I'm so good."

She hands me the ball and my fingertips graze hers. She winces as somebody turns up the volume on the music.

"I just realized that all I know about you is that you dislike loud music and can't play hockey for shit."

She rolls her eyes. "What would you like to know?"

Where have you been all my life?

"Is that house . . . where you live . . . all the time?"

"I live in Manhattan. Upper East Side. I grew up in the Village. I'm just here for a month."

"Wow. So you're actually from New York?"

"I am."

"That must have been so strange, to grow up there."

"Not really. It's all I know. Where are you from? A frozen lake somewhere?"

She tosses the Ping-Pong ball. This girl is sinking every shot.

"What's your last name?" I ask.

"Riley."

"Is that your married name?"

She stops and stares at me. "It's my name name."

I can't bring myself to inquire directly. At this point, I don't even care.

"So is Harlem really a dangerous place?" I ask.

"No. There's a Rao's."

"What's a Rao's? Is that like . . . a Mafia thing?"

"It's more of a tomato sauce thing."

I toss the ball and it clunks off the edge of a cup. I try to think of another New York question.

"Is the pizza really that good?" I ask.

She gives me a long look, like I'm a fucking idiot, but then she starts to smile. "In some places, yes. I'm partial to the Village places. But it really depends on what you're looking for. John's on Bleecker has the best pies, with toppings. Onions and meatballs, if you're serious, and I think that you should be. If you're looking for a plain cheese slice, I'd go to Joe's. But not just *any* Joe's. The Joe's on Carmine Street. But you can't get it delivered or purchase the slice and then leave. You have to eat it there, *within the establishment*. Seriously, if you take it a few blocks away to Washington Square Park, you're eating something else entirely."

I am amazed. "I should write this down."

"You absolutely should," she says. "You never left college to come to New York?"

"No," I say. "I didn't have any money. So what's your book about?"

"You can't ask a writer that."

"Why?"

"Think about the plot of any book or movie. In isolation, it always sounds idiotic."

"Try me."

She sighs. "It's a retelling of *Ulysses* as a romantic comedy, about a girl in college who wants to sleep with her James Joyce professor. It takes place in modern day but there's a lot of Greek mythology feathered throughout. Basically, it's playing with the classic 'hero' story of *The Odyssey*."

"So it all happens in one day, or what?"

"You've read *Ulysses*?"

"I know the general plot. I'm not a total blockhead, Jessica."

"I didn't say you were."

Who knows how many beers later, she is about six inches in front of me and I'm watching the bottom of her dress sway as she moves. It's taking all my powers of restraint not to take one step forward.

"That's a nice dress. You aren't fucking around in that dress."

"What's that mean?"

"You know exactly what it means."

She shrugs with a smile. "I grabbed the first thing I saw."

"Well, it's working for you."

As time goes by, I am inching closer and closer to her. Before she takes her next shot, she stops, looks back at me, dark hair covering most of her face.

I freeze. I am two inches from having my arms around her.

She opens her mouth, eyebrows raised, and says: "Can you move?"

I don't know. Can I? I move my head closer to her face, pretend that I can't hear her. "What?"

"You're crowding me," she says, in a low voice.

"Oh. Sorry." I back away, our eyes locked.

"Are we playing a game here or what?" our opponents yell from across the table.

"Sorry, guys! I was just telling Carter how my back is hurting . . . from *carrying* the team."

I am amazed at how nothing is awkward with this girl. She rolls with everything, gets along with everyone in the room. My mind is flooded with calculations. *Don't go in for the kill tonight. Play it cool. Don't come on too strong. Just get her number or make a vague plan and then you can follow up later. Ask her more questions about herself, then break it off, disappear, act aloof, leave her wanting more,* which is a perfect plan except that she smells so good and everything in my body is screaming *now, now, now.*

"Oh my god!" A girl approaches Jessica. "Are you Jessica Riley, the author? I loved your book so much!"

"Yes!" Jessica says.

"Okay," the girl says. "Stop everything. I need the inside scoop on how you came up with the character of Ben. He is so boyfriend goals! Is he your husband or something?"

I hold my breath. A girl comes up to me to ask if I can FaceTime her dad. Apparently, he's a huge Rangers fan. I do it so that I can pretend I'm not listening to Jessica's conversation, but I am. I have my eyes one place, and my ears another.

"No. No. Just a totally made-up character," she says. "A little bit of this person and that."

"Are you writing anything new?"

"I'm working on my second novel now."

"That's so exciting! How's it going?"

She laughs lightly. "Okay . . . I came out here to concentrate, which is working . . . somewhat."

"Do you live in the city?"

"Yeah!"

"Me too! That's so funny! Whereabouts?"

"Upper East Side."

"Oh my god! *Me too!*"

Well, well, what do you know. And then I hear a roar from the other room. My friends are freaking out over something. Jessica and this girl move across the room. I go to see what all the fuss is about.

A penalty call has turned into a fight. Crosby is pretending he got hit in the face. "Look at this fucking faker," somebody says.

"Yeah, that's exactly what he's doing," I say. "But so what? He's trying to win the Stanley Cup. Get the fuck out of here—faking. What does that even mean?"

"It means play the game! It's not *honorable*. It's disrespectful. Total bullshit. He's done this before."

"Yeah, so? He didn't invent it."

The third period is over, and the game is going to overtime. We are all glued. I am watching but also searching for Jessica in the crowd. I am scanning scanning scanning for brown hair and a white dress. Then I spot her and breathe a sigh of relief. She's still talking to that girl. It's fine. She's still here. She's occupied. I am praying she doesn't leave, a bead of stress running up my spine.

I turn to Harps and say: "All right. Who's going to score the overtime winner?"

"Crosby," he says.

"No," I say. "It's going to be Max Talbot. He always plays his best in the most crucial moment. He's not afraid to run into the fire."

The Penguins score in the first two minutes of overtime—Crosby indeed—and win the Stanley Cup. I lose myself in watching the celebration. The greatest trophy in sports. And then, I lose Jessica. I look around the room. I turn to Harps.

"Have you seen Jessica?"

"No . . . but you know she's married, right?"

I can barely hear him. I'm too busy scanning the room.

"Carter?" he says to me. "HELLO?" I don't answer. He grabs me by the shoulders to get my attention. "Are you going after her?"

Carter?

Hello?

WHY?

I look at Harps, the TV screen, then back at him. "What do you mean 'why?' *For the love of the game*," I say.

He is silent.

I walk around the house, which is more difficult now, as it's gotten even more crowded. Jessica is nowhere to be found.

She probably left. *Fuck*.

I push through all the bodies and check every room and can't find her anywhere.

I go outside to smoke something, drown my sorrows.

And there she is, by the pool, talking to JT. They're both laughing. Well, I wanted her before, but now I have to have her. And it has to be tonight.

She touches her fingers to his chest, pushing him slightly. He pretends to fall dramatically backward. Hamming it up as always. But every girl at this party is the same to him.

My body is tense, operating without my control. I can feel a knot inside of me, threatening to expand, the slight vibration of my bones. I walk up to them.

"Hey," I say to him, not looking at her. "Can you take out the garbage?"

He stares back at me. "Absolutely. Give me ten minutes."

They are clearly in the middle of something, and there is nothing left for me to do but walk away. In my walk of shame across my own house, I am wondering if I've played this all wrong. I feel my irritation rising, a poison needing to escape. I think about that damn book. *Chapter 7: Tackling Daily Life: Any reaction you have to anything that's above a six is a reaction to something else.*

Ten minutes? Okay. Ten minutes.

I push my way through the crowd and go down to the basement where it is quiet. I put on Nirvana. "Lithium." I set the boxing clock that we keep in our basement for training to ten minutes. The oversized clock begins to count down, the numbers in menacing red.

I stand on the synthetic ice and fire pucks into the net. I am hitting them hard. I am starting to sweat.

I shoot until I hear the buzzer and see the 00:00 flashing.

Time's up.

I rush back upstairs. Back outside to the pool area. But I can't find JT or Jessica. To get my heart to slow down, as I move about the room, I do one of my exercises.

Identify five things you can see . . . a blue hat, an open window, plastic cups, lit cigarettes, smoke.

Four you can touch . . . my jeans, the hair on the back of my neck, the hard bone at the top of my nose, the skin on the inside of my palm.

Three you can hear . . . the bass of the music, people shouting, sportscasters on the TV.

Two you can smell . . . beer, sweat.

One you can taste . . .

And then I see her, walking through the sea of bodies that is our living room, toward the door. I need to get to her before she leaves. Luckily, it is difficult for her to get through. She is moving slowly. I push people. I make my way. Once I'm behind her, I get as close as I can, until I can feel the temperature of her skin, and then I run my hands down the side of her body, her waist, hips, the sides of her legs. She turns.

6

JESSICA

I CAN SMELL HIM BEHIND ME. I recognize the scent of his clothes, his skin, from earlier. There are so many people, so many bodies, but I still know it's him. When I feel his hands on my body, I turn, pretend not to know. He pretends he doesn't know either. He stands there innocently, a blank look on his face.

I stare at him, shake my head. *No.* I turn. I keep walking. A few seconds later, he does it again. Quickly this time, I turn. His hands are in his pockets. He stares back at me. I keep walking.

The third time he lingers for a few seconds, motionless behind me, and I stop. I can't move either. What I want to do is turn around and lick his skin. My body is humming. I'm feeling the pleasure so deeply. Too deeply. But I force myself to snap out of it, and then I keep walking toward the door, at a faster pace. I have my wits about me now and I know what to do: Lose him in the crowd.

I duck and weave and in no time at all, I am out the door, relieved at the night air. I look at the line of parked cars in the driveway, imagine myself shimmying past each one, the way I did when I got here. *No. Too slow.* I decide to cut through the woods this time, to make a run for it. All I can hear now is the muffled sound of the party and the crunch of my flip-flops against leaves and tree branches. All I can feel now is my own heartbeat.

I'm halfway through the woods when I hear somebody running behind me. I pick up my pace. I can see my house now and I go toward it like a beacon of safety. When I get to the line between our properties, I go sideways through a row of trees, covering my face with my hands so that my eyes don't get hit with any branches. I sprint across my driveway, open the front door and then close it, slam it shut, keel over, one hand on the door, breathing heavily at the ground. I press the door and turn the lock. I take a nearby chair and drag it in front of the door, for extra protection.

I take out my phone and put it on the kitchen counter, so that I can't be reached by anyone, then run upstairs to my bedroom. I close the door so that I can't hear anything beyond this room. I lock it.

I get into bed and let my breathing even out, wait for my heartbeat to settle. I count my inhales and exhales until they steady. I hear a knock on the front door. Maybe. Could have been a knock. Could have been something else. But then it happens again and I'm sure. I am not answering it. I am not going anywhere.

I take off my dress, bra, and underwear and put them on the

floor next to the bed. I lie there naked. I put my fingers inside my body. They slip in easily because I'm so wet. I have to press hard to get any traction. It is like rubbing out a stain that you want desperately to go away. I hear the sound of more knocking. Louder now. I close my eyes and suddenly, we are at the party again. Except this time he's whispering in my ear, all the things he wants to do to me but can't. I want him to be frustrated. I want him to be going out of his mind. He is.

There is more knocking. I am moaning to the sound of his hands on my door. My hips are beginning to lift. The knocks get louder. I overcome them with the sound of my own voice as I start to come, and then, picturing his eyes above me in the dark, come harder.

7

CARTER

The shades are pulled down and I'm lying on the couch in a robe, eating salt and vinegar chips out of a bag. There is an open container of weed gummies on the table next to me as I watch game one of the '94 finals. Rangers versus Vancouver.

People come and go. They ask me questions, but I'm in a fog, barely listening. All I can do is lounge on the couch, lie in bed, or stare into space. I'm thinking about the past, daydreaming about the future. I'm replaying conversations and inventing new ones. My mind is going far off in different directions, but none of those directions is here on Earth.

JT's sister, Jill, is over. They are standing next to the couch, evaluating me like a specimen in a lab.

"What's wrong with him this time?" JT asks her.

I mumble: "That Alexei Kovalev was soooooooo slick."

Jill says: "Isn't it obvious?"

JT shakes his head.

"He's bent out of shape about a girl."

I call out: "Ohhhhh. The Moose is loose!"

Jill says: "What's he talking about?"

JT stares at the TV. "Messier."

I'm not looking for a diagnosis. I know exactly what's wrong with me. It's very simple, you see. I am . . . how do I put this lightly? Fucked up. Yes. I am royally fucked up. I've woken up from fist fights and felt less banged up than this.

I am jamming my hands into my forehead a lot throughout the day, closing my eyes and trying to shake it off. *You gotta shake it off, man.* It's nothing. *Nothing* happened to warrant this reaction. I don't know how I got this way. I don't know why this one girl is affecting me so much. But it's not within my control. It's like a bad pill that hasn't worn off yet. I embarrassed myself last night. It made me feel weak. I can't be weak. I need to act like a pro.

Harps tries to make me feel better by quoting Shakespeare. He comes over to me with a book. He reads: "Misery makes sport to mock itself," and then he closes the book dramatically. "Richard the Second," he says.

"Thanks, man, that's . . . very helpful."

"Just leave him alone," Jill says. "He'll snap out of it eventually."

But JT doesn't want to leave me alone. He wants me to go to Pilates.

"*Dude.* Come *on.* Svetlana and Nicole are taking the eleven a.m.! We gotta be there. We don't have time for one of your mood swings."

I get up and go into my bedroom and lock the door and lie in bed and stare out the bottom half of my window. Then I close the blinds completely and take a nap and wake up two hours later.

"No. No. Absolutely not. You are *not* bringing him to this party," I overhear Jill say to JT. "He's not a staff member! And he's not a guest! There's a list. This is a very exclusive event, maybe the most exclusive event of the entire summer. Do not fuck this up."

I hear the door close. I leave my room.

"Put some clothes on," JT says to me. "We're going to a party."

"I'm not going."

"Oh yes, you are. What the fuck, bro? You heartbroken over our neighbor? Are you gonna sit around and lick your wounds all day? Let's go meet twenty hotter and richer girls. It's the Fourth of July, for Christ's sake!"

I roll my eyes. "Fourth of July."

Harps adds: "Actually, the Fourth of July occurs during a significant period, astrologically. It's the day before the new moon."

"Oh, well, that changes everything," I respond.

"Come *on*," JT says to me. "It's the party of the summer. Some billionaire throws it. I heard Tom Brady is going to be there. Beyoncé. Joe Burrow. Megan Fox. Jay-Z. Zach Bryan. Ice Spice. Leonardo DiCaprio. In a *fifty-million-dollar* house. By the end of the night, you won't even remember her name."

"How am I going to get in? I'm not on the list."

"Dude! This party is all professional athletes and New Yorkers. You're about to play for the *New York Rangers*. This won't be a problem."

Harps surveys the room, the bags of chips and weed gummies surrounding me. "I'll say this. It won't help you to stay here."

I rub my forehead with my hands. "Yeah . . . Okay. I'll go."

"When we get there," JT instructs me. "You just walk right in like you own the place. Somebody is going to know you. And put a smile on your fucking face. Loser."

There are paparazzi stationed outside the property's manicured hedges. A long lineup of catering trucks and black SUVs. We are at the back of the line, in JT's Toyota, the two of them in their catering uniforms of white jeans and white T-shirts.

"Jesus," I say, examining several tents full of photographers.

We pull into the driveway, a long and narrow pebble road enclosed by hedges on both sides. We can't see the outside world, but we are eventually spit out of the green maze, and before us is a beachfront mansion, a glass rectangle with multiple patio decks. We can see the ocean through the living room.

JT and Harps head off to the catering tent. I walk up to the two women standing near the front door.

"Your name," one of them says to me, with raised eyebrows. I tell them.

She scrolls through her phone, searching for answers. "We need the passcode from your invitation." She clears her throat. "The personalized Nikes."

"Passcode?"

"Yes." She is exasperated. "On the tongue?"

"Carter Hughes!" A guy behind her yells. He motions for me to come in. I have no idea who he is.

The girls are still staring at me. But I blow past them.

"Ohhh, you know what? I think I gave those away," I say, looking back at them. "I don't want to wear anything the kids can't afford."

One of the women smiles. The other one is still exasperated. I walk up to the man that has summoned me.

"Carter Hughes!" he declares. "PK was supposed to come, but he canceled at the last minute, so this is great. At least we have somebody from the hockey community."

"Happy to sub in," I say. "Tom Brady told me this party is a must."

He nods, affectionately. Any friend of Tom's.

"The house is composed of eight glass cubes," he says, starts pointing around.

"Wait. This is your house?"

He nods. "It certainly is."

"How often do you clean the windows?"

He laughs. "Why? Are you looking for some extra work?"

"Yeah, but it'll cost you."

He laughs again. "I heard you were a wild card."

I follow him.

I've never seen anything like this before. Such obvious wealth and decadence. The abundance of glass and light makes it feel like being inside and outside at once. There is a staircase in the center of the house that is clear, as is most of the furniture. Furniture so expensive that you can't even see it.

The tables are covered in gold vases and marble orbs and the occasional gathering of white candles. The chandeliers are large, strange, made from hundreds of lightbulbs or butterflies or masses of green hair. There is a long, glass-enclosed fireplace running down the center of the living room. On the walls are gigantic paintings of blonde models in seductive poses, and one photograph of an oversized Popsicle melting into concrete. He talks about architects and artists as if I've heard of them. I haven't.

We go outside. The patio is adorned with velvet beanbag chairs and ottomans that look like large stones. I'm imagining what it must be like without all these people, all serenity and spa-like, but right now the house is draped in girls wearing skimpy white dresses showcasing their bodies, the fabric barely clinging to their breasts. One girl is wearing a white dress with a gold metallic belt encircling her waist like a serpent. Another has on a see-through white beaded dress with a hood. The guys are in white T-shirts, their necks covered in diamond crosses, layers of gold and silver chains. I see Prada triangles everywhere, like tiny stamps of authority.

"Go and have fun," the host of the party says to me, once the tour is over. A woman in a white bathing suit and sheer skirt, presumably his wife, requests his attention.

He puts one hand on her shoulder. "Honey. This is Carter Hughes," he says, "He's going to play for the Rangers this season."

She reaches out her hand to shake mine. "That's so exciting! You must be on top of the world."

I smile. "Absolutely. I am. But the job isn't nearly done. I've gotta help bring a Cup to this town."

"That's what we like to hear," her husband says, patting my back.

"Well, you're not going to win a Stanley Cup tonight. So just try to enjoy the festivities. And laugh!" she says. "Laughter really is the best medicine."

"Thanks. I'll remember that. I'll remember to laugh."

I take the wooden path to the beach. There are tents set up on the sand dunes. I see JT and Harps going back and forth between them, collecting trays, bowing their heads as they approach people.

"Wagyu beef with a truffle sauce," Harps says.

"Summer tomato salad," JT offers.

I stare out at the water for a while, mesmerized by the glory of my whereabouts. JT pretends to be serving me tomatoes but then starts narrating. He points at an elderly man with wild white hair and a white beard. The man is stacking firewood in the sand. "That's the famous chef from Argentina. The one who only cooks outdoors."

I start walking down the beach. There is a tent labeled *NOBU*. It smells like garlic and soy sauce. In another tent, there is a large circular pan filled with meatballs and tomato sauce. I look at the awning: *RAO'S*. Another reminder of Jessica. Constant reminders of Jessica. *Fuck Rao's.* I keep going.

"Carter Hughes!" I get stopped by some Rangers fans. We talk about how the season is going to go, some of the other guys on the team, the coach.

I talk to a bunch of finance bros, then some football players. They all seem to know who I am. It's great. I don't have to say anything. I just stand there, smile, nod, watch all the beautiful women. I've never seen this many models in one place.

There is a bar set up on the beach. I order a drink. A famous singer approaches me. Her husband is a famous actor. A real celebrity power couple.

The bar is not crowded, but the singer places her hip alongside mine. "Can you order me a drink?" she asks.

"Sure," I say.

"You look like an athlete," she says.

"I'm a hockey player."

"Oh my god! I love hockey! I'm Canadian! Wait right here. You need to meet my husband."

He comes over. I've never seen a couple like this in the wild. The two of them proceed to try to get me to go back to their house.

Am I being lured into a threesome? What the fuck is happening?

I am not drunk enough to accept but I am drunk enough to think about telling this story to my friends later and get a kick out of that. Like money in the bank. I feel good, suddenly, and completely rid of whatever has been plaguing me. I am firing on all cylinders. Gaining friends left and right. Making people laugh.

I look across the party at JT. He has taken his uniform off, has a white wifebeater on. He's off duty now, with his heart set on a blonde gymnast. Harps is with some yoga chick that everyone seems to know.

The sun begins to set. Everyone goes up to the roof of the house, which is a tennis court transformed into a nightclub. There is a dance floor and a stage, all lit up in pink.

A dance party breaks out. The musicians in the crowd, mostly rappers, give impromptu performances. I dance with random girls. Three or four of them give me their phone numbers. This may be the greatest party I've ever been to. *This is where you belong.*

Once the performances are over, the house music kicks in. Waiters pass by me carrying mirrored trays. One with white powder. One with powder that has a slight pinkish hue. Pink cocaine, JT says, doing lines with the gymnast. I watch people put it on their gums.

A series of lights shoots up from a barge in the distance. We go to the edge of the roof. A dazzling pattern appears in the sky. Everyone sighs and applauds. After the fireworks display, people are hoping for the appearance of a humpback whale. Apparently, he surprised everyone last year. But the whale doesn't arrive. Some animals can't be bought.

We leave at five in the morning with a bag full of bagels. A parting gift. We drive to the beach and watch the sun come up.

"You see," JT says, holding up a cinnamon raisin. "This is what real money can buy. People slinging bagels at five in the morning."

"What a terrific night," I say, taking a bite of mine.

"Well, I think I won that party," JT says. "That gymnast is the hottest thing I've ever seen. And she's calling me tomorrow."

"Like hell you did," I say. "I have ten or twenty DMs from girls at that party."

"Did you not see that yoga instructor?" says Harps. "She was a prize. I think she might be married too . . ."

"The gymnast is a fucking celebrity!"

"A celebrity." I laugh.

"She is! She's one of the highest paid female college athletes in history. She was on the cover of *Sports Illustrated.*"

I say: "You know what we need to do . . . "

"What?"

"We need to keep score."

JT smiles at me: "He's back."

On the car ride home, we debate the details of a points system based on categories. "So it's points per conquest?" Harps wants to know.

I say: "I'm thinking something more elaborate than that." Back at the house, we search for writing implements. "Where should we write it?"

"I got it," I say, remembering that one of the kids' rooms has crayons in the desk drawer. Crayons that write on glass.

I take the pack and go toward the sliding glass doors that lead to the pool.

"Are you insane?" says JT. "Everyone will see it there. *Girls* will see it there."

"There's a full-length mirror in my room," Harps offers. "On the inside of my closet door."

We take the crayons to his closet. Each color indicates a different category. There are eight crayons.

1. *local hot girl (townie) or bottle service girl*
2. *female athlete*
3. *yoga teacher*
4. *fashion influencer*
5. *model*
6. *musician*

7. *татTV or movie star*
8. *billionaire's daughter*

"We sound superficial," says Harps. "Women will think we're disgusting."

"We are disgusting," I say. "But so are they. They do this all the time."

"That's right. I'm looking for a man in *finance*," JT says, and then starts singing the song. Not really a song. A TikTok sensation involving a girl who wants a finance guy with a trust fund and blue eyes.

"What's worse?" I add. "Us wanting to fuck models or them wanting to fuck finance guys? We're not trying to reinvent the laws of attraction here. We're all animals."

Harps says: "Maybe there should be bonus points for a woman who, in addition to beauty, has some substance."

"Get the fuck out of here," JT replies.

I say, "Harps, you go ahead and bag an archeologist. You have my permission. And good luck finding one at a party in the Hamptons."

8

JESSICA

I INVITE MY FAMILY TO COME stay for the weekend because it's ninety-five degrees in the city and at this point the guilt is killing me. On Friday night I meet the car in the driveway as it rolls in. Both kids are in pajamas, asleep in their car seats. Alejandro removes four suitcases from the trunk.

"How long are you guys staying?" I ask, jokingly, but I know. Four suitcases is nothing with kids. Two days. Easily.

Alejandro lifts our son over his shoulder and then follows me into the house.

I show him the room with two beds that I set up for them. He puts our son into one bed and then goes back to the car for our daughter.

There is no designated "kids" room, but I created one. I bought stuffed animals and a moon nightlight at a toy store in town. I took all the star-spangled blankets and pillows from all over the house, along with a few lanterns with electronic candles that were in the kitchen, and made the room look like a cozy, upscale campsite. The result is adorable.

Our son is out cold, but our daughter wakes up long enough to hug me and look around at the room: "The world is so beautiful today. You're a really nice mom." Then she is asleep, and I am feeling vindicated.

"So how does this compare to your business trips?" I say, as Alejandro examines the house. "In terms of accommodations."

"Larger," he says. "But no housekeeping. Or room service."

"That's right. I have to make my own bed. It's dreadful."

"Neighbors still loud?"

"Oh! I went to their party the other night."

He looks delighted. "How was it?"

"It was interesting . . . Would it not help you to go to a party with a bunch of twentysomethings in your line of work?"

He grunts. "The twentysomethings getting paid to work in my office don't help me with my line of work."

He goes to the sliding glass doors, puts his hand over his eyes, squinting at the dark. "I never have my own pool."

"You should request one. Highly recommend."

I toast two pieces of bread and cover them with butter. We talk about the kids. Talking about the kids with Alejandro while they're asleep is one of my favorite activities, because we are almost always laughing while we do it. And also they're asleep.

We go upstairs. He unpacks. I take a hot shower, so hot that I emerge from it in a puff of steam, my feet slightly red.

He is already in bed and holding the remote. I put on boxers and a T-shirt and climb into bed. I notice that my pillow is missing.

"All right. Where is it?"

He smiles. Hiding my pillow is one of his favorite moves. There is a huge lump under his side of the comforter.

"You're so clever." I jerk it out from under the blankets. "How would I have ever found this?"

He laughs maniacally and turns on the TV, clicks on *30 Rock*. He scans the episodes.

I pull the covers up to my nose. "Now. Where were we?" I ask, shimmying my body close to him and throwing my arm over his stomach.

"Did you watch any since you've been here?"

"Not a single one."

"You're so good."

"I am so good."

In the morning, I wake up early and make pancakes for everyone. Banana pancakes with chocolate chips, to be exact. I sprinkle some oats into the batter and put only three chocolate chips per pancake. That's right. Nutrition.

I cut up strawberries and a mango. The mango is difficult to cut. Berries are one thing, but a mango means true love.

They all wake up and join me in the kitchen. After breakfast, they want to go for a swim.

My daughter screams for me to change her into her suit. She is standing there naked. "You are five years old! You know how to put on a bathing suit!" I tell her.

"I want you to do it," she whines.

"Okay. Okay."

I get them in their suits, apply sunscreen, locate goggles, towels, floaties. What feels like a decade later, I am with both kids in the pool, my daughter chasing the colored rings I bought her at the store. My son is shooting and refilling a water gun, repeatedly. We are waiting for Alejandro to change into his bathing suit, which for some reason always takes forty-five minutes. But eventually he arrives, tosses both children into the air on a rotating basis, water splashing everywhere. They are both positively tickled with glee.

The pool is a glorious place where everyone must live in the present and get along and nobody can ask Mom or Dad to get out and go bring them something. The servants are off duty. Life becomes very simple. Splash or be splashed. I try to get some laps in, but Alejandro keeps swimming after me, grabbing for my ankle and taking me under. The kids get a big kick out of this and call the game "daddy shark."

I get out of the pool first so that I can lie in the sun for a bit before going into the kitchen to make fish tacos. I never cook, but this seems simple enough. I bought all the ingredients at the market yesterday and have grand plans to put all the toppings in separate small bowls. I am sure that separate small bowls and choose-your-own-toppings will greatly enhance the chances of the food going into my children's mouths, but it's anyone's guess.

I bake fish in the oven, slice corn off corncobs, dice tomatoes and onions. I execute on the separate bowls. It's all going swimmingly. Pun intended. I can see the pool from the kitchen window, and I admire my family, the way Alejandro can play with the kids for hours without seeming bored or annoyed.

Eventually, they come inside.

Alejandro surveys the kitchen table. "Look at you," he says.

"Are you impressed?"

"Very."

"Are you impressed . . . or do you want to check me for signs of a concussion?"

"A little of both."

My daughter fills her taco with fish and corn and tomatoes and happily eats the entire thing. My son stuffs his face with only lettuce, a stunning move no one could have anticipated.

"After lunch, I was thinking we could go to . . . a carnival? I don't know if that's the type of thing you'd be interested in," I say to my daughter.

"*Yes!*" She lights up, pumps both fists and smiles so big that you can see every one of her missing teeth.

"You want to go to a *carnival*?" Alejandro whispers to me, gritting his teeth at the kids.

I shrug. "I haven't been parenting lately. I have an unusual amount of energy. This is the kind of magical thing that can happen when you give me some time off. Please, make a note of it."

Once they finish eating, I make a quick run to Carvel, return home, and remove two ice cream sandwiches from a six-pack. I wrap the sandwiches in a napkin and then present each child with one. My daughter gasps. My son's eyes light up like a contestant that has just won a million dollars. Sure, I've been absent for a few weeks, but it's nothing some flying saucers can't fix.

We get ready for the carnival with all the items we need to survive life outside the house with kids for two hours, which is considerable. I fish through my backpack, overflowing with fruit snacks and Goldfish and pretzels, to hand the car keys to Alejandro.

I go to the bathroom and tell him: "Put on their shoes while I'm gone, okay?" He nods. When I get back, they're still shoe-less.

"I thought I told you to put on their shoes?!" I say.

"I'm talking to them about it."

I sigh and go get the shoes. You know that Buddhist expression about parenting? There is no difference between talking and doing except when it comes to putting on their fucking shoes.

In the car, my son sings GA-GA-GA to the tune of "Hot Cross Buns." He is a broken record. We try to get him onto another song. We, as a family, sing Taylor Swift and Carly Rae Jepsen and various Disney hits, like a bunch of lunatics, but nothing works. By the time we get to the carnival, we give in. GA-GA-GA, GA-GA-GA.

When we get there, my spirits are high. Maybe not high. Decent. But it is not long before I am standing in a hot field, using a baby wipe to remove cotton candy from my sunglasses. Our son has been crying for almost the entire time. Our daughter is melting down not because her pizza is hot but because it was once hot.

"The five-second rule applies to pacifiers, right?" I ask Alejandro as I wipe dirt off our son's pacifier. It has just fallen onto the ground for the fourth time.

An hour later, we've gone on five rides and played three games, but I've run out of snacks. I find a cheese stick. The only problem is I can't remember when I put it in my bag.

"Do you think it's still good?" I ask him.

"What does it say?"

"It says the expiration date. It doesn't say what to do if you leave it in your backpack for eleven days."

Our son is crying.

"Just give it to him," Alejandro says, and I unwrap this string cheese as if my life depends on it, which, in some ways, it does.

"Okay. I've had enough," I say to Alejandro, looking down at my sweaty, red-cheeked children. "And I think they have too. Let's go."

"Are we walking home?" my daughter asks, gripping my hand as we cross the field.

"No. The car is here."

"Phew. What a relief," she says.

You're telling me.

For dinner, I make pasta with butter, and they eat in front of the television. I say a silent prayer of thanks for the invention of television. I go into my bedroom and lie there, exhausted, relishing the quiet. I am in a state of euphoria. Sex is great, but have you ever taken your kids to a carnival and then come back and read a book alone in a quiet room? It's really something. Quite exquisite.

Alejandro comes into the room.

"I can't move," I say. "Please don't make me move." He plops down next to me.

"I just came here to tell you one thing."

"What?" Suddenly, I'm nervous.

"GA-GA-GA. GA-GA-GA."

I cover my face with my hands and roll over onto my side, laughing.

"I have a question," I say, craning my neck to look up at him.

"I've come to fear your questions, but go ahead."

I sit up on the bed, cross my legs under me. "Since the kids are busy with camp and things seem kind of slow for you at work right now . . ."

He is sighing already. He knows me too well. I push through.

"If I start taking the train into the city on the weekends . . . Maybe I could stay here for a few more weeks . . . or so . . . Just to get this book done. I mean, I'm over halfway done, I might as well, right? I have the house until Labor Day, and it's been working . . . being out here, without all the distractions. So I should just bring it on home, right? Don't you think?"

He sighs again, more audibly this time. He can't question my logic. It is airtight.

"I suppose."

I am trying hard not to grin widely at the kindness this man has bestowed upon me.

"I'll take the train into the city on the weekends," I assure him.

He starts laughing. "You said that already."

"No, but I really will. I'm not a horrible mother. Please don't call the authorities."

"I'll try to resist."

Despite the freedom that I've just arranged for myself, when I watch them drive away the next day, back to the city, I feel a pang of sadness so deep that I almost start to cry in the driveway. I want to chase after the car. I want to end all of this. But I tell myself that I just need time to adjust back to being alone. The discomfort will pass. Alejandro calls me from the car, and we chat for a bit and I realize that they aren't gone forever.

I go outside for a swim in the late afternoon light. I grab a towel and head to the pool, which suddenly feels very quiet.

I put one foot in the pool and then jump out and scream at the top of my lungs.

There is a long green snake in the water. It's slithering around, its head bobbing up and down at the surface. It is desperate to get out.

Well, I can't swim now. I'll never swim again.

"Everything okay over there?" I hear Carter call from the other side of the bushes.

I stand there silently, recoiling in horror. *Not him. Not him. Anyone but him.* I don't move. I am waiting for him to go away. A few minutes pass. I'm still frozen in place.

Then: "Hello?"

Damn.

"Yeah!" I yell back. "There's just a snake in my pool."

"Jesus. I thought somebody died."

"No . . . it's still . . . very much alive."

I start to squeal, unable to control it any longer, and back away from the pool. I know how I sound. But I can't help it. A frog would have been okay. Even a mouse. But a snake I can't handle. It occurs to me now that it'll die in the pool and then I'll have the same problem tomorrow, with nobody around.

I sigh. "Do you think . . . you could get it out for me?"

I hear his garage door opening. He arrives with a net attached to a long rod.

An hour later, the snake has been flung into the bushes, and we are sitting on lounge chairs with beers.

"Were those your kids? I thought I heard them in the pool over the weekend."

"Yeah," I say. "For once, I was the one with the noise."

We sit quietly for what feels like a long time.

Finally, he says: "Did you hear Harps on Saturday night?"

"No. What did he do?"

"He had a wild night. Three girls in the hot tub."

I gasp. "I can't believe I missed that." I smile. "I guess he says very few words, but they're all the right ones."

"He had a ten-point night."

"A what?"

"Come on. I'll show you."

I follow him to his house. Inside, the guys are on the couch, watching something on TV. He shows me into one of the bedrooms and opens the closet door. I stare at the mirror full of colored writing. He explains it to me. The system.

"I think this may be the craziest thing I've ever seen . . . Is that crayon?"

"Don't worry. It's washable."

"Oh yeah. That was my concern."

I take out my phone. Start typing in the Notes section.

"What are you doing?" he asks.

"I'm writing this down."

He laughs. "You are?"

"If you're going to do something *this* insane, I'm sorry, but I'm going to have to take it from you."

He makes a sweeping gesture with his hand. "It's yours."

I finish writing and then stick out my hand to shake his. "Nice doing business with you." He smiles.

We go back into the living room. They are watching 9½ Weeks. "I remember this movie," I say.

"Sit down," Carter says.

I sit and watch for a little while with them. On screen, Mickey Rourke puts an ice cube in his mouth and lets the freezing water drip all over Kim Basinger's body. She is squirming with pleasure.

"Oh yeah. That's realistic," I say. The guys are mesmerized. I click on my phone to check the time. "It's late. I should go."

"Okay," Carter says.

"Stay out of the freezer, boys," I say as I stand. I turn to Carter. "Thank you for showing me the system."

"Oh, you're welcome."

He follows me, stands there holding the knob of his front door. I stride down the driveway.

I turn back and smile, say: "Good luck out there." I widen my eyes at him, and he widens his back at me.

Damn. He's cute.

9

CARTER

It's pitch-black outside and we're crawling on the highway, inching along on the trail of cars trying to get from Southampton to Montauk. I'm drumming my hands against the steering wheel, trying to keep it together, but after four straight days of weight training at the Southampton Gym, I'm raring to go, to have some fun. So is JT.

"Come *onnnnnnn*," he says.

I jerk my car to the right and start driving on the shoulder. If anyone has a problem, we'll get out of it. The Rangers' head of security, a former NYPD chief, gave me a card and said: "If you have any issue on the East End, call this number."

JT turns to Harps. "Tonight . . . is the beginning of your downfall."

"I doubt it," he replies, says nothing more.

JT looks at me. "I was impressed with your political moves last weekend."

"The Hamptons, man," I say. "You fuck around with some girl named Barbara and next thing you know, you're having breakfast with two former presidents."

"I still don't believe you didn't say anything stupid."

"We mostly talked about hockey."

"That's convenient. You know what? I trust you in that situation. I trust you with political dignitaries . . . You make a good first impression. I worry more about your seventh impression."

"I'm not seeing Barbara seven times." Under my breath, I say: "I could barely drive to Amagansett with her." JT laughs.

We ride the shoulder for miles on 27, the two-lane highway connecting the entire East End of Long Island. We drive to some dark part of Montauk, end up at a club, its name, DREAM EAST, lit up in neon blue.

When we get inside, the electronic music is thumping and the bottle service girl that JT has been texting is standing in the crowd, somewhat near the entrance, eager for him to arrive. He goes up to her and she whispers something into his ear. They head straight to the bathroom to blow lines. We might not see him for the rest of the night.

There's a VIP table in the back waiting for us. A few pretty girls are sitting on a velvet couch. I get introduced to a girl wearing a thick diamond choker and a yellow dress. Every strand of her long hair appears to be a different shade of blonde. A silver bracelet is halfway up her arm, gripping just below her elbow. On both wrists are stacks of colored beads, along with a watch that looks expensive.

"I'm Charlotte," she says.

She's awfully dressed up for a club in a surf town. As we talk, she cocks her head to the side, lifts her chin when she laughs. It's as if she's posing for photos that aren't being taken.

"I hear you're going to play for the Rangers!" she yells over the music.

"Yup."

"What a dream come true!" she says. "You must be so excited! I've heard you're a bit of an instigator. Or is it an agitator? What do they call it?"

I smile. "The life of the party."

She nods. She is all cheer, so much cheer that I fear I don't really need to be there. She is really getting into the music. She knows exactly what to do. It feels a little rehearsed. Her friends dance with her. They are holding hands and taking photos. Selfies. Videos. TikToks. They ask me to take some and one of them instructs me to hold the camera up high. I take a bunch as they change the tilt of their heads and smooth their hair and adjust their arms—hands on hips, peace signs, pursed lips.

The longer I stand there taking photos, the happier they become. They yell out compliments, tell me what an excellent Insta-boyfriend I would make. I hand the phone back, and Charlotte eagerly scans the photos but seems to have mixed feelings about the results. While they evaluate, JT comes up to me. He looks completely waxed. *Gone.* I don't know what the fuck has happened to him in the past half hour.

"Do you know who that girl is?" he whisper-screams into my ear.

"No. Who is she?"

"That's Charlotte Chapman. Her dad is the CEO of Chapman Smith. She's a model and an influencer and a billionaire's daughter." He widens his eyes at me. "You do the math."

I raise my eyebrows and I do.

He takes out his phone, looks up her Instagram. He hands it to me. @caratsandcashmere. I find out that Charlotte is a girl hawking diamond-encrusted cashmere sweaters. Charlotte is a girl who owns a store in the West Village. Charlotte is a girl who attends a lot of flower-filled dinner parties at long tables with her name written in script on the menu.

I look at her latest photos. A picture of a sunset. *The most magical place. Grateful.* A bowl of pasta and a glass of wine. *Dinner and dancing every night and lots of gelato! Incredibly happy. #TomatoMartiniSummer.* Italian flag. Pasta emoji. A video of her hair being blown out, followed by a close-up of a handbag. *So grateful.* A piece of fish and a bowl of mashed potatoes on a dark plate. *Home away from home.* A picture of herself in a body suit in a bathroom mirror. *Best most exhausting weekend but so fulfilled.* A shot of her in a bathing suit with two other girls. All three of them are wearing the same sunglasses. They're all posed the same way, arched backs, chins up, lips pursed, leaning into each other like swans. *À la mer.* French flag. Croissant emoji.

"What did you learn?" JT asks, taking his phone back.

"She's very grateful."

"Yeah. No shit."

She drags me onto the dance floor.

"The summer is flying by," she screams into my ear. "*Flying.* We live by the beach. Do you like the beach? I *love* the beach.

And my family! I just adore my family. They're like my rock. The most loyal, supportive, loving family I could ever ask for."

I stand there as she takes numerous selfies with me, turning her face in different directions and changing the position of her lips. She will do anything to get a good shot. She is shameless. *It's my business*, she is prepared to say to anyone who might question it.

Her friends approach her. They convince her to leave. There's another party. I'm surprised by her sudden departure. As a consolation prize, she tells me that they're going to Sunset Beach tomorrow night.

"What's Sunset Beach?" I ask.

"*What's Sunset Beach?*" She laughs. "Oh my god, you have to come! It's a restaurant-slash-bar-slash-hotel on Shelter Island. You'll love it. You have to take the ferry to get there, but it's *so* worth it. It's a really pretty ride. Great for photos."

The next afternoon, the guys and I drive to Sag Harbor. Again, we're riding the shoulder. This is what we do now. This is how we get around.

We wait for our turn to drive onto the ferry, each car ahead of us slotting into position, guided by a man wearing an orange vest.

"So, this is a hotel? There's a hotel on an island in the Hamptons?" I say to JT, who is looking out at the water.

"A few. More like glorified motels with fancy shit in them. Speaking of hotels, I forgot to tell you guys. You know that girl from last night? She brought me back to her hotel. The Dunes in

Amagansett. Anyway, we start making out in the hot tub. Turns out you're not supposed to be in the hot tub after eleven or whatever, and there are security cameras, so some bellhop comes out with a flashlight."

We start to laugh. The ferry churns beneath us.

"But she can't find her bikini bottoms. They are nowhere to be found. So being the chivalrous man that I am, I just throw her over my shoulder, and we book it to her room."

Harps laughs. "God, I'd love to see the face of the employee who found her bottoms floating in the water this morning."

We drive off the ferry and onto Shelter Island, which is much quieter than Sag Harbor. It feels remote and secluded, with not a soul in sight and very few cars on the road. Between all the hedges and shrubbery, you can get a glimpse of the impressive houses. It is quaint but wealthy, the type of wealth that has been here for a while. Every store looks weathered. Some parts of the island are more manicured, but then you go around a bend and the landscape becomes untamed.

As we drive, it feels like we're alone on this island, until we get to Sunset Beach, which is humming with people and music. We pull into the parking lot, right next to a row of rooms with private porches, overlooking the ocean. The rooms are attached to a two-story building, open on all sides. We get out of the car, pass by people playing bocce on the sand. Across the road and closer to the water, there are bicycles, paddleboards, and chairs set up next to yellow umbrellas. It is like an upscale playground for adults. I can hear people speaking different languages. We can feel the wind in our faces. It smells like oysters and the ocean.

We walk up the stairs to the rooftop, where people are eating at tables and gathered at the bar. It's completely open, with yellow chairs and orange tables and strings of lanterns hanging overhead, strewn from one striped pole to another.

I spot Charlotte in the crowd.

"Hey!" She comes up to me and gives me a hug. She is wearing a white polka-dotted top with a black polka-dotted skirt and carrying a cup of something yellow with a slice of pineapple attached to the rim of the glass. "You made it! You *have* to try this drink. It's the best. It's called a BVI Painkiller."

"What's in it?"

"I don't know. Rum . . . pineapple, and orange juice. Makes you feel like you're in the Caribbean!" She adds: "I just got back from Italy, actually!"

"Wow." I feign amazement. This is brand-new information. "How was that?"

"It's the most stunning, magical place! I want to move there!"

She introduces me to her friend, another influencer, who goes on and on about her new line of body mists.

"I *just* announced that I'm launching them, and I've been dying to show everyone!" She takes out her phone. "I've been traveling in Europe. We just got home. I've been *obsessed* and *living* in these. Obviously, I'm in my golden era." She laughs. "Look at the bottle!" Charlotte oooohs and aaaahs. "How cute is it? It has that cute little glitter, you see? Shells, oh my god, *star fish*, it's all *so* delicious I honestly can't stop spraying it. This is what I've been, like, *living* in all summer long. They are *so* delicious! I'll definitely send you some!"

I order a Painkiller, to kill my pain. Charlotte takes a picture of us all clinking glasses. We have to do it several times before she gets the shot.

"Tell me more about Italy," I say, once the booze kicks in, pulling my barstool up close to her. "I'm sure you took some great pictures."

She shows me some. I start to zone out and scan the restaurant. That's when I see Jessica, sitting at a table. I feel a burst of new energy, good energy, and a sudden enthusiasm for these Italy photos I'm looking at. My responses to Charlotte become more animated.

I keep glancing up. Jessica is sharing a piece of cake with someone. She looks natural in this environment. They are engrossed in conversation. I am so immediately jealous of this woman sitting across from her that I want to lasso this friend of hers across the room while she's sitting in her chair.

Charlotte gets dragged away by some famous DJ she knows from high school. Harps catches me looking across the room. "Hughes," he says. "Don't be an idiot."

"I know."

"Don't be a fucking idiot."

"I know. I know. Just get rid of the friend, okay?" I say to him. He pauses. We stare at each other.

He sighs. "Okay."

We head over to the table. Jessica sees me. She is smiling. She is tipsy. Perfect. Harps leans down toward the friend: "God. You're beautiful."

I crack up.

"I'm married," she replies, giving him an amused look.

"I can appreciate that. Let me buy you a drink," he says.

She looks at Jessica.

"Go have a drink," Jessica says. "It *probably* won't end in divorce."

Her friend gets up and Jessica is left sitting at the table with nothing but an empty wine glass and a tall goblet full of ice.

"Well, look who it is," I say. "My neighbor."

She puts her elbows down on the table and gives me a glaring look, like *What do you want?*

"Can I sit?" I ask, pulling out the chair.

"I don't think I have much of a choice."

"Good instincts," I say. "What's with all the ice?" I take the glass and put it in front of me. I examine her face, her cheeks slightly red from too much sun. She is wearing a white tank top and jean shorts. No makeup. No jewelry. Her legs are crossed under the table. I can see beige sandals with straps that wrap around her ankles. Just sitting across from her is turning me on.

She explains: "I don't really like wine, so I ask for it over ice, but they don't want to do it." She rolls her eyes and flips her hand in the air so that her palm is up, motioning to the glass. "They give me a glass of ice so that I can do it myself."

"Well, it's like ordering steak and eating it with ketchup."

"See. *That* I wouldn't do."

"That's where you draw the line?"

She smiles. "That's where I draw the line."

She stares at me, looking like a wave of discomfort has hit her. But then I realize that it's not discomfort. It's fear.

I reach into her glass and remove two cubes of ice. I put one in my mouth and crunch down hard. I keep the other in my hand. I put my hands under the table. I reach to see how far away her crossed legs are. I graze one of her shoe straps with my fingertips. *Right there. Easy.*

"How was your dinner?" I ask.

I hold the ice cube against her ankle, just above the straps, and run it up her calf slowly to the back of her knee. She sits there very still, her eyelids lowering slightly.

"I don't know," she says.

I feel like these are my legs, like I touch them all the time, like they belong to me. "You don't know?" I ask. I don't even know what I'm saying.

She shakes her head.

"Interesting." I brush my thumb along the inside of her knee.

Once the ice melts, I press my hand against the back of her calf and hold it there. She inhales sharply. Then she exhales and the sound of her breathing is making me hard.

We drift into a place where we aren't really talking. I put my hand on top of her knee. It is smooth, slightly bony. I feel around, extend my fingers, draw them back, each new part of her skin giving me another pang of hunger.

She looks around, then clasps her hands together as if she's about to start a conversation. But she doesn't say anything. I am feeling her calves up and down because the thighs feel too dangerous. Anything above the knee is going to put me over the edge.

"I'm not . . . unhappily married, you know," she says. I couldn't care less. Nothing exists beyond this table.

I lean in and say: "Can I ask you a question?"

She almost rolls her eyes, then stares at me, leans forward. I move one of my hands to the inside of her thigh. I expect her to flinch, to push me away, but she doesn't. I get close to her ear, close enough that strands of her hair are in my eyes and nose: "Are you happy now?"

And then she sits back and grips the table with both hands and pushes it hard against my chest. The force of it is so hard that I have to work to keep my chair from falling backwards.

She stands up, blows past me, and goes to the bar. I get up and stand there watching, so stunned that I can't even move. *What the fuck was that?* At the bar, JT has ordered a tray of shots and is passing them around to a group of girls. Large girls. Tattooed girls. Not-from-around here girls.

I see Jessica approach the tray.

She removes a shot from the tray, downs it, scrunches her face up in disgust. She looks up at me and then turns away. Her friend joins her, points to some other people at the end of the bar. Jessica waves at them.

I go closer to the bar.

I watch as she downs another shot.

"Jess!" her friend yells, and then laughs. She looks at her friend and shrugs. Her friend slinks past the bodies huddled at the bar, ends up bumping into one of JT's girls, spilling her drink.

"*Excuse me,*" the girl says to Jessica's friend. "Girl, you are *not* hot enough to be standing so close to me."

"Sorry!" Jessica's friend cries out.

Jessica turns around. "*What did you just say?*" It's unclear why she is suddenly yelling. "Because she spilled your drink, you're insulting her *looks*? It was an *accident*. Chill."

But Jessica is the one that needs to chill. She is messing with the wrong crowd. These girls are twice her size. These girls will kill her, and the reason I know this is because I hear one of them say: "I'm gonna kill this bitch."

The girl lifts a shot from the bar and pours it on Jessica's sandals. Jessica screeches and looks around for the nearest object, which is in the hands of the bartender—a lime that he is about to slice. She grabs the lime and throws it at the girl. They all duck and laugh. Jessica is reaching down, unraveling her sandals, about to take one off, presumably to throw it.

Still in disbelief, I push into the crowd and reach for Jessica and lift her up. I carry her down the stairs and out of the bar, as she kicks wildly at my knees with the one sandal that is still on her foot. The other one is in her hand and slung over my shoulder, dangling by its string.

I put her down on a bench.

"You're starting bar fights now? Are you fucking nuts?"

"She was rude to my friend! How dare she insult her looks! My friends are *all* hot! All of them are hot!"

I start to laugh. She's drunk. Her friend has followed us down the stairs and crouches down beside her.

"Jess." She shakes her head. "What is going on?"

Jessica looks down. "Nothing. I'm fine."

"You just threw a lime at a stranger."

"Oh, will you guys *relax*? I'm *fine*. Everything is *fine*. They dodged the lime. Let's go party." She gets back up and starts to climb the stairs.

"Jess!" her friend calls. "I'm going home."

Jessica stops, looks at her friend and then at me.

"I can give her a ride," I say to her friend.

"Are you sure?" she asks Jessica. "Jess, why don't you just come with me? It's late. We should go." The friend is wary.

Jessica hesitates. "No way. I'm not going back to that empty house. Not yet," she replies. "Text me when you get home, okay?" she says to her friend and then turns away.

Upstairs, the bar area has transformed into a dance party. Shots are being passed around. Girls are dancing on the tables. Jessica is ignoring me and goes over to the group of people she knows and sits down with them.

It's a bunch of guys in white linen shirts, khaki pants rolled up. Their wives are all dressed in white and pink dresses, with stacks of gold and diamond bangles on their arms. I decide that they must be telling stories about their families. Jessica must be talking about her weekend with her family, how they came to visit her during her wild solo time in the Hamptons.

What would I have to add?

You're on completely separate paths. Pursuing her is pointless. Worthless. Zero points.

I look at her from across the room and somehow manage a warm feeling about letting her go. I have to get used to it. I'm sure it won't be the last time we see each other out. Tonight, she was meant to be with her older, sophisticated New York City friends, sipping cocktails. And I was meant to do tequila shots at the bar with JT and an influencer who wants to move to Italy.

Charlotte is after me and honestly, I have to respect the hustle. She keeps asking me to dance. She doesn't let me out of her sight, except once when somebody hands out sparklers and she and her friends take them down to the beach for a "barefoot dance party."

I indulge her. She is cheerful and fun, and by fun I mean she is almost always jumping up and down with her hands in the air. So I dance. I take more photos. I need a break. I grab her by the shoulders.

"Do you want to just sit in the sand for a little bit?" I say. "Or smoke a joint?"

"Okay," she says, slightly dejected. "Hey," she whispers, touching my elbow and then moving her body in close to mine. "I have something you might be interested in."

"Oh yeah? What's that?"

She rifles through her handbag and shows me two keys attached to shell-shaped silver coins. The coins read *Sunset Beach. Room 301.*

"I got a room. Just in case I wanted to crash."

My heart is pumping as I look down at Charlotte in her diamond choker and white polka-dotted top. You can see the outline of her breasts. She puts one key in my pocket.

I don't exactly say yes, but once she decides to leave, I follow. JT and Harps see me walking behind her toward the door. They're pissed. They know that this is big. They'll have to work to catch up.

We walk down the stairs. As we cross the parking lot, Charlotte loops her arm into mine, pretending to be drunker than she is. Suddenly, she's wasted, giddy.

I look back at the bar, up to the top floor, where a girl is standing with her hands on the railing, the wind whipping her hair as she stares back at me. It's Jessica.

10

JESSICA

I AM GOING TO BE *SICK*. I'm surprised by how bad I feel, by how fucking horrible it makes me feel to see him leaving with that girl, that soulless polka-dotted creature in a diamond necklace you can see from outer space. My only plan is to get the fuck out of this bar and head toward the water. The water will save me.

I walk down the beach, away from the crowd near the hotel, to a part of it where I can be alone, where nobody can see me, and then I feel a wave of nausea. I bend over. I expect to throw up, but I don't. I stand there for a while, wait for my body to feel somewhat stable again, then sit on the sand, cross-legged, looking out at the water. The sunset has thinned out to just a strip of red. The sun is a half-circle, glowing above the Peconic Bay.

I don't feel like myself at all. It's been a while since I've felt the acute sting that occurs after this kind of hit. Everything in my life has become a little off since I met him. It has all faded into the background, making space for this onslaught of emotions. Little Miss Jessica. Little Miss Breaks the Rules found someone who really knows how to break them. Serves her right.

I sit there, lost in my own thoughts, for what feels like an hour. I sift through my history with other guys, try to make sense of what is happening here. I take out my phone and fill the Notes section with a deluge of emotions.

I've flirted before, but this time is different. The temptation is too strong. My heart rate is too elevated. I've always had control. I'm always sitting comfortably at the switchboard, pushing buttons. Now I feel like the victim. I write: *It's like looking out at a rough ocean, knowing that if you step in, just a little, you'll drown.*

Well, I've had about enough. I need to just stay away from him. That's all. That's the only answer. Separation. Distance. Avoid him at all costs. It shouldn't be too hard. He's with another girl already. I doubt he'll ever seek me out again.

And that's when I look to the right and see him walking toward me, his feet lifting a clump of sand with every step. Despite all my resolutions, relief floods through me.

"You know what we have to do," he says, sitting down next to me. "We have to teach you how to throw a punch."

I smile but can't look at him.

"In case there isn't any fruit available."

I shake my head at the sand.

He says: "Okay. Stand up. Stand with your feet shoulder-width apart."

I hesitate, then do as he says.

"You're right-handed?"

I nod.

"Put your left foot forward and your right foot slightly back. Keep your hands up and your elbows close to your body."

He holds up his hand and I try to hit it.

"Okay . . . that was . . . terrible. Use your hips and shoulders. Your whole body. You're only using your arms."

I try again.

"If you engage your core and legs, you'll generate more force." I do it again and nearly fall over in the sand. He laughs.

"Oh my god. What's wrong with you? All you're doing is tightening your fist. Extend your arm straight from the shoulder."

I hit his hand as hard as I can.

"Better. Try to make contact with your knuckles, not your fingers or the palm of your hand. Keep your wrist straight and snap it slightly. Then take your arm back so that you're ready to throw another one if you have to."

We do this a dozen times. Then we sit down and quietly stare at the water. I use a stick to make marks in the sand. He is propped on his elbows.

I ask: "How often are you fighting people anyway?"

He looks me over. "What do you mean?"

"*What do I mean?* I've done my research."

He is still for a moment. "You say that like I'm fighting random people on the street."

"*Aren't you?*"

"Sometimes." He laughs. "I've been praised for it my whole life. I did what the other kids weren't doing. I tried to hurt the goalie on the other team, which was somewhat unusual. I played in a peewee tournament on Prince Edward Island in Canada, and when we took the ferry back with the other team, and I terrorized that team so much during the tournament that the parents on both teams made me ride back up in the captain's quarters, away from everyone."

I narrow my eyes at him. "What's your problem?"

"It's a great question. I don't know. I always had the ability to turn a tournament upside down, to cause fights in the stands, in a hotel. I was enemy number one at age twelve."

"Is this the result of a traumatic childhood?"

"I don't think so. My parents were always pretty calm. The first time I got in trouble was in first grade, when I made fun of a deaf kid in our class."

"*Why?*"

"I didn't believe that he was deaf. I started yelling and clapping, trying to startle him."

"That's horrible!"

"I don't know what I was thinking. I probably didn't understand the concept of someone being deaf. I also bit my mother in the parking lot of a Chuck E. Cheese when I was eight."

I nod. "I used to bite the other children on the playground. There was one redheaded girl that I was always after. It got so bad that when the other mothers saw me arrive, they would take their kids home. I had a reputation."

"When I was sentenced to my room, which happened often, I used to take a tennis ball to bounce off the walls and I would do it for hours, trying to drive my parents insane."

"If I asked my mother if we could go to the bodega to buy candy and she said no, I would lie down in the middle of Broadway."

"*Jessica . . .*"

"I know. I know. I was such a menace."

"I had to get out of there," he says. "Everyone thought of me as this dangerous outcast. But at least on the ice, I could tear the place apart, cause complete chaos. They could try to kill me, fight me. But that was helpful to my team. And I was rewarded for creating chaos."

"You're not afraid of the consequences?"

"No. And I'm not afraid of physical pain either."

I raise an eyebrow at him. "You left yourself wide open there."

"I did?"

"Well, now I just want to ask about the emotional pain you're so afraid of."

"Good luck getting an answer."

"Seriously. *What is your problem?*"

"My parents never told me they loved me?"

"That doesn't seem like enough of a reason."

He laughs. "It doesn't?"

"You'll have to be more specific."

"My dad was the same if I won or lost. A few words. Never a big reaction to anything."

"Oh. Well, I can imagine that being frustrating."

He looks at me, at my mouth, then down at the inside of my thigh. He says, "I have this recurring dream that I'm in my sixth-grade classroom, and the teacher and students are all there and they see me, but they aren't engaging with me at all. They're just calmly going about their business, as if I'm not there."

I stare at him, studying his features in the almost-darkness.

"This is my nightmare," he says, shaking his head. "Not that I'm being buried alive or chased by some maniac with a gun. I'm just basically . . . being ignored. And I wake up in a cold sweat. At least if you provoke somebody, they might care enough to punch you in the face."

I laugh. "You want your presence to be felt."

"Not everyone can be the one provoking people. But I can, so I make use of it."

"Sometimes a professional strength is a personal liability. Many of my romantic monologues are fueled by some rage I felt about something else. People will say to me: Why are you *so* *angry*? I'm trying to make something of myself. That's why. *Why aren't you angrier?*"

"I know," he says. "No rage? Good luck trying to be successful at something that many people want and most can't have. I'm trying to not end up back in Johnstown. It's not that I don't want to be derailed. It's that I can't be derailed. *Sorry* if what fuels me sometimes flies off in the wrong direction. *Sorry* that I'm not in complete control of it at all times. It's not a perfect world. I'm not a great humanitarian. And I never claimed to be. That's somebody else's job. I am a force."

I lie back, bend both knees, dig my toes into the cooling sand. "I had the president of a literary agency once say to me: 'You might be a good writer, but that doesn't mean you have to do it for a living. It's hard and you'll never make any money, so if you don't *have* to do this, you shouldn't.' I looked him dead in the eyes and said: 'I *have* to do this.' And then he agreed to be my agent, and I marched right out of his office and into an alleyway on Seventh Avenue and pumped my fist and screamed, 'Come on!' at the top of my lungs."

He laughs at me. "God."

"It was so loud that a flock of pigeons flew away." I am laughing with my eyes closed. "A homeless man ran in the opposite direction."

"I'm trying to think of a consistently even-tempered person who I'd like to hang out with for more than two seconds."

I turn onto my side. "Speaking of which . . . what'd you do with that girl? The girl with all of that . . . blonde hair?"

"She's not my type."

"No? She's pretty . . . rich . . . What's not to like?"

He shrugs, like he's tired.

"Plus . . ." I pause for dramatic effect. "Phenomenal tits."

He gives me a serious look. "I know."

"Do you think they're real?"

"They seemed fake to you?"

"They just seemed a little far apart, like one tit had nothing to do with the other. There was no togetherness, no synchronicity."

"You could be right."

I say: "She'd make a great evil villain actually, with that choker . . . She had antagonist written all over her."

It's late. Our friends are long gone. The hotel guests have retired to their rooms. We can hear the waitstaff shutting down the restaurant. We are the only ones outside. Suddenly, I am creeped out by the silence, the pure darkness.

"You know, if you murdered me right now, nobody would know," I say.

"If *you* murdered *me*, nobody would know." He brushes sand from his legs. "Death by sandal."

I laugh, cover my face with my hands, stand up, dust the sand off my body.

"You know you can never show your face here again," he says, looking up at me.

"Oh, I'm sure they've seen worse."

"I'm not." He stands up. I give him a slight shove as we walk.

"All right," I say. "How are we getting home?"

"We're not going home." He raises his eyebrows and then removes a shell-shaped key from his pocket. "We're sleeping here."

I gasp. "Is that *her* room?"

He shrugs. "I doubt she's using it."

"How can you be so sure?"

"Because I hurt her feelings, and she has a house twenty minutes away to drown her sorrows in. The room was just a ploy."

We walk away from the water, toward the road.

"I'm not having sex with you," I say.

"I know that. But come on. I'm exhausted, aren't you? And it's right here. Let's go check it out. I promise you don't have to have sex with me."

"You need to write that on your forehead."

"For you or for me?"

"For both of us."

The room is sparse. A white bed with a wooden headboard and matching wooden nightstands next to it. There is a glass table in the middle of the room with an orange and white beach ball on the floor. I look at the bed.

"You take it," he says. "I'll sleep on the floor."

"What? Really?"

"I can't lie in that bed next to you. I will try to fuck you. Guaranteed."

"Fine. Take a pillow at least."

I put the pillow on the floor next to the bed and grab a blanket that I find in the closet. He already has his head on the pillow when I put the blanket over him.

"Are you okay?" I ask.

"I'm okay."

I get into bed. Under the covers, I remove my shorts and bra, let them drop to the floor. I pull the covers up to my nose and lie there, completely still. I stare at the ceiling, listening to him move below me. Then I shuffle my body toward the side of the bed. I dangle my arm over the edge. He takes my hand and holds it. I must have taken it back at some point, but I don't remember when.

There is a loud knock on the door. It startles me awake. Carter gets up to answer it.

"Good morning, sir. Sorry to bother you, but we found these at the front desk. We believe they belong to you. Your friends left them."

"Thank you," he says, in a raspy voice, and then closes the door.

I sit up, hold the covers to my chest. "What was that?"

He coughs. "My car keys."

"They didn't take your car?"

"I thought they would. I gave them my keys. I guess they found another way home."

"You mean we could have driven home last night?"

He looks at me. "I'm glad we didn't."

"Me too."

On the ferry ride home, he opens the windows halfway. I look out at the land in the distance, the large houses overlooking the water. I listen to the steady hum of the boat as the water churns against it. His left hand is on the steering wheel. His right hand is resting on his thigh. I put my head on his shoulder, then wrap my arms and hands around his right arm so that the entire thing is in my possession.

I laugh. "Can you drive without your right arm?"

"I'll let you know if I need it."

11

CARTER

THE HARDEST PART IS LETTING HER out of my car. Once I put the car in park, I say nothing, just place my hand out in front of her, palm up, and she holds it. My fingers weave into hers.

I say: "If you're not going to give me this hand to take with me, then can I at least have your phone number?"

She pauses, stares out the window. "*Fine,*" she says, as if I've asked her a million times.

I plug it into my phone like I've never done this before, careful to get everything right.

Under name, I put *Jess*. Because we're friends now. She can't tell me that we're not.

She gives me a hug, or what limited hug can be given across a center console, and when I breathe into her hair, I can't believe I'm not kissing her. She leaves and closes the door, and I still can't believe I'm not kissing her. I just sit there stunned, unable to move. I watch her at her door, searching her bag for her keys. I stare at her legs and the straps of her shoes and feel a wave of regret.

A minute later, she's still searching for her keys. I get a rising sense of hope that she won't be able to find them, so that I can extend this a little longer. *What a predicament! Can I offer you some sex?* But then she finds them, turns to wave, almost but not quite looking at me, and goes inside.

For the next few days, I am attached to my phone like an appendage. I am thinking about texting her with every thought that comes into my brain. But I don't.

"She's right there!" JT yells, pointing to her house. "Just go over there and fuck her."

"I can't," I reply.

"You see. He wants her, but he can't have her," explains Harps, to an imaginary crowd.

"He's being a pussy," says JT. "That's all this is."

At some point it dawns on me that JT is right. I am being a pussy. I find her number and press *Message*. I think for a second about the wide variety of nonsense I could say, but it all feels beside the point. Fuck it. I'm going in.

Sat, Jul 20 at 2:57 PM

> I was really hoping you wouldn't find your keys

> Honestly . . . me too

> I miss you

> Shouldn't you be training?

> Yes, I should but I can't concentrate. You want to come over and watch me shoot pucks?

Get real

Sat, Jul 20 at 10:07 PM

> Did you ever play any sports, besides beer pong?

Tennis. I was actually pretty good, nationally ranked. 75th in the country, when I was 16.

> I guess that explains the hand-eye coordination. Did you play in a skirt?

Yes... but not a matching shirt. The girls with matching outfits were weak.

> What type of underwear did you wear with your skirt?

I'm not telling you about my underwear!

> If we played doubles together, could I pat you on the ass if you hit a good shot?

Maybe

Mon, Jul 22 at 9:24 AM

Who's in the lead these days with that stupid game you guys are playing?

> Harps and JT are tied at 24

And you?

> You're not telling me about your underwear? I'm not telling you about my points

Why?! I really want to know

> No, you don't

Ok fine I don't. At least tell me if you're winning or losing

> Losing

Mon, Jul 22 at 3:58 PM

> What are you doing?

Reading. I just read a sentence with the word ha in it, so I'm all burned up

> Why?

Don't say ha in literature!

> Sure. Why not just go for the lol?

It's deplorable

Tue, Jul 23 at 10:13 AM

> People are serious about their farm stands here

Lol I know

> Have you been to Amber Waves?

Yeah

> What's the big deal?

No idea. People like the hats, but I think they're overdoing their allegiance. It's not a lifestyle! It's a farm stand

> You are cute

Wed, Jul 24 at 12:38 PM

> I bought your book in town today

Are you gonna read it?

> What if I don't like it?

Then we'll never speak again

> What?! Really?

I once cut a guy out who read something I'd written out of order

> You're crazy

Crazy like a writer

Thu, Jul 25 at 9:28 AM

> Did you know that the oatmeal at The Golden Pear is $14?

Doesn't surprise me.

> Maybe it's special

> It can't be special. Nothing at that place is special

>> You're right. My dad used to make me "special toast"

> What was so special about it?

>> It had butter, cinnamon, and sugar

> Cinnamon toast! A classic. My mom used to make me toast, and it was either white or black. There was no in between

>> Child abuse

Thu, Jul 25 at 9:20 PM

> I'm watching Dirty Dancing. I watch it once every summer and you know what? It never fails me

>> Are you thinking about me?

> No, I'm texting you for some other reason

Sat, Jul 27 at 10:39 PM

>> How's the writing going?

> Pouring out of me now. Go figure

>> Can I be your muse?

> Yeah, but it's a lot of work

Sat, Jul 27 at 11:47 PM

Are all hockey players like you?

No. I'm a misfit

I feel like a misfit but with writing

Why? You're a successful writer

Yeah, now. But before, there were 99 rejection letters, and they all said the same thing: I don't fit into a category. I'm not heavy enough to be literary and not light enough to be commercial. "We don't know what shelf she would go on in the bookstore"

That's infuriating. Pussies

But why fit into a category? What's the point? I'd rather fail doing it my way than succeed doing it just like everybody else.

I understand. If I were just a great offensive player, things would be a lot easier for me. But I play hard and mean and do whatever it takes to win.

You gotta play the way you wanna play!

You gotta. And a good coach will never try to fit you into a category. They'll just . . . well, in your case . . . build a new shelf?

Right. But not everyone thinks this way. Publishers want to take what has worked in the past and go down that same road again.

Want me to burn down their houses?

Would you?

Mon, Jul 29 at 10:20 PM

Look out your window

Why?

Trust me

Holy shit. Are we being attacked?

By what? Stars?

Why are there so many of them though?! Maybe those are airplanes?! They look ominous, all spread out and blinking???

They can't be airplanes. They aren't moving

One is

Okay maybe one is an airplane

It looks a little crazy, but beautiful

I just wanted you to see it

I never stop to look at the stars

That's because you're a savage

Tue, Jul 30 at 12:24 AM

Are you still up? Just got home

I actually am. Writing. Can't stop. I keep imagining my Pulitzer acceptance speech, in case you have mistaken me for a sane person

I think to be really good at something, you have to have delusions of grandeur.

Of course. Those are the dreamers. Those are the ones that win, that don't stop.

I need an enemy to perform. Even if I've conjured the whole scenario in my head

I used to sabotage myself as motivation, like if there was a lull in the season and I needed to pick myself up, I would do something that I wasn't supposed to do so that I would go out and play harder.

I dislike a lull

Tue, Jul 30 at 10:02 PM

Tell me something nobody else knows

I was once locked in a locker room from 1 AM until 9 AM.

Seriously?

> We were out at a bar in a rival town thirty miles away, the night before a game. Our coach got a call that we were there and he was pissed, pulled us out of the bar, drove us to the arena, brought us into the locker room as if we were going to have a meeting, and then locked us in. By 3 AM, it was probably minus twelve degrees in the locker room and we thought we were going to freeze to death.

That's terrifying.

> You get used to the pain.

I went to a tennis training camp in Florida in August, and I got heat stroke and had heat rashes on the backs of my legs, so they taped ice packs to my legs. I played for a week in 95-degree heat with heat stroke and heat rashes on half my body and ice packs taped to my legs. But by the end of the week, I was fine. I felt like such a warrior. It was a good lesson that everything becomes less painful over time.

Tue, Jul 30 at 11:15 PM

Carter.

> What?

Nothing

> Tell me

It's nothing forget it

> Tell me

It's nothing!

> It isn't

I'm just really into you

> That's nothing?

Yes! Forget I said anything!

> PLEASE let me fuck you

No. I'm going to sleep. Gnight.

Thu, Aug 1 at 9:48 AM

> We're going to the batting cages in Yaphank. Only 45 minutes away

Impressive. I've got a real cereal / TV situation going on here

> What kind of cereal do you like?

How much time do you have?

Thu, Aug 1 at 8:38 PM

> I just want to know what you're wearing right now

Hahahahaha get real buddy

> UGHHHH

> Scream into a pillow or something

>> I just did. Didn't help

>> Can I get a visual? Seriously I'm about to break out Harps's telescope and then there's no telling what will happen

> How far does that telescope reach? I'm in the city right now

>> You are?

> Yup. This is NYC Jessica. Do I sound different? Edgier? More urban?

>> Kind of. Text me when you're back

> I will.

Sun, Aug 4 at 10:42 AM

> I had a dream about you last night. I was so disappointed when I woke up

>> I hate that feeling

> I don't know. It felt pretty amazing. Before that

>> Jessica

> What?

>> I really want to fuck you

Mon, Aug 5 at 2:47 PM

What are you doing tonight?

I'm meeting my agent at this event, Authors Night. It's "the premiere literary event of the Hamptons" which is funny because the Hamptons has no other literary events

What happens there?

Well, it's a field with a tent and a bunch of books under it and people pay $150 to chat with authors and get their books signed. There's a dinner afterwards.

Can I come?

Absolutely not.

12

JESSICA

I AM DETERMINED TO GET BACK to my life. I feel like I've been under water, trapped in a whirlpool of text messages and fantasy. I need to come up for air. To get out of the both literal and figurative bed I've made for myself.

So I write. I research. I FaceTime my children, compliment the bracelet my daughter made, laugh as my son bangs on a toy car with a rocket launcher. I arrange playdates and sign them up for after school programs for the fall. When I come home on the weekends, I take them to the ice cream museum and the safari playground in Central Park, and when I leave on Sunday night, I tell them that one day they'll be proud to have a mother who isn't a one-hit wonder.

My book is almost done. My agent is thrilled. I don't feel quite like myself, of course, because I'm doing nothing but working and thinking about sex with my neighbor. That is my whole life, and my whole life is this. But I keep sending pages to my agent and he keeps telling me how good they are, so I keep going, addicted to the praise, like a junkie.

I don't leave the house but I'm on the phone with people all day, conducting interviews, gathering information. Swimming laps whenever I have frustration to burn. I have written the majority of this book in a bathing suit.

Tonight, I am finally attending something official. I am going to an event in East Hampton, Authors Night. My agent calls beforehand with some last-minute details.

"I'm bringing two hundred copies of your book," he says. "Get ready to sell."

"Two hundred? How am I going to sell two hundred books in two hours?"

"You sold that many last year. You sold them, and then I believe your exact words were: 'I'm a hustler, baby, don't try to change me.'"

I sigh. "Bring the copies."

I scan my closet for something author-ish and land on a light blue one-shouldered dress. It is knee-length, appropriate. I put my hair in a ponytail rather than leave it down because it's a thousand percent humidity, and if shit is going to hit the fan, I like to get ahead of the game, hair-wise.

I look in the mirror. I feel a little dressy, considering I have been spending most of my time in either a bikini or sweatpants. I slip on sandals. I'm out the door.

I already feel better on the drive over. I'm about to go somewhere. I'm about to do something. This is nice. This is *normal*.

I pull into a field full of cars and roll down my window to find out where I should park. The attendant motions for me to go next to a vintage white Lamborghini with Florida plates. The car has a bumper sticker that says GRANDPARENT PARKING ONLY *all others will be towed.* Authors Night really brings out the heavy hitters.

I approach the big white tent. I pose for some photos. They give me a wristband and tote bag and bring me to my table, which is in a long row of tables, each with stacks and stacks of books on them. My agent is there unloading a cardboard box.

"I'm glad you're here," I say, and give him a hug. "I was about to knock over a thousand copies of *The Light Between Us.*"

He stops unloading and stares at me. "Just because you blurbed her book and she didn't blurb yours does not mean you should be out for blood."

"I firmly disagree."

Before the signing begins, we take a stroll around the tent. There is no food but many ice buckets filled with drinks. Montauk Brewing Company is the sponsor of this event. So I sip from a can and go from table to table, checking out the books and letting my agent introduce me to people.

"This is Min Jin Yong," he says, when we approach one table, but he doesn't need to say that. I know who she is. She's won multiple Pulitzers.

"Jessica Riley," my agent says to her, motioning to me. "Jessica is one of my authors." She shakes my hand, looks amused.

"She's not an author," she says. "She's a model!"

I laugh. "Yeah, except for my face," I say, and then puff out my cheeks. My agent puts his hand on his forehead. "*Thank you.*" He looks at me, annoyed. "What she means to say is *thank you.*"

He corrals me away. "What are you doing?" he whispers to me. "That's Min Jin Yong."

"I was just making a joke! You know . . . Because models have visible cheekbones," I say, sucking in my cheeks now. "They look like this." I look at him with my cheeks drawn in. "And I'm just a regular person. With cheeks." I grab one of them.

He looks at me and is about to laugh but stops himself.

"Pull it together," he says. "Be normal, just for the next hour."

"Okay . . ." I say. "But that's really not why you hired me."

A line begins to form at my table. We go toward it.

"Oh my god! *The Light Between Us* chick has already sold half her table."

"Sit," he says, handing me a pen. "Sign. We don't have time to delve into all your archrivals."

I take the pen and raise my eyebrows. "We should *make* time."

He rolls his eyes. I plop myself down and start signing books, chatting briefly with people. Some are excited to read, some have read and are taking a copy for their friend or daughter or nephew. Some lift the book right in front of me, scan the cover, rifle through the pages, and just keep on walking.

"It's *fine*!" I yell after them. "No hard feelings!"

My agent laughs. "You need to *relax.*"

I scoff at this. "*You* put your soul on a page and then relax!"

He introduces me to editors, other agents, magazine people. The woman sitting next to me signing books is the former editor-in-chief of *Glamour*. She is hawking a book called *The*

Love Diet. She is pretty drunk and has no idea who I am. She keeps taking photos of my book and promising me she has a big following on Instagram, that my book is going to be huge someday. *Huge*. I look down at the top of my book, where it says: *#1 New York Times Bestseller*. Apparently, she can photograph the book, but she can't read it.

Suddenly, I feel a little lightheaded, and I don't know why. I have a prickly sensation in my chest. I look up and across the room, I see Carter.

He's at the opposite side of the tent and my heart immediately races. *Is he serious? Why can't I get away from this guy?*

He does a lap around the tent and then sees me, gets to the back of the line. My hand is shaking as I make small talk with an elderly woman named Gloria who has been trying to be my agent for years. She's a bit of an oddball, talking to you until the cows come home, right up in your face, but she always has the best publishing gossip, so I like her.

"Serves her right," she is saying. "Trying to leave Knopf for all those years. They finally called her bluff."

Once Carter is at the front of the line, Gloria is still bending my ear about the state of contemporary fiction.

"You came," I say to him, mocking the voice of a girl who might be desperate for him to show up. I roll my eyes.

"I'm not going to miss this," he says.

"What's the matter? Couldn't stand the fact that some people might want *my* autograph?"

"That's exactly why I'm here." He slaps the book down in front of me. "Sign it, Riley. Make it a good one. Include a short poem, would you?"

I roll my eyes again. "Haven't you gotten enough of my messages?"

As I'm signing, I look up at the crowd gathered around my table. "This is Carter Hughes!" I tell people. "He's going to play for the Rangers!"

It is silent.

Carter stands there waiting. They look mystified.

"The Rangers . . . " Gloria says, putting her hand under her chin. "Is that what they call the Parks Department in New York?"

I widen my eyes. "It's a hockey team!" I say. "They play at Madison Square Garden! Come on, Gloria!"

"Sorry." She laughs. "I'm not much of a sports fanatic."

As she leaves, I hand Carter the book. "Don't sweat it," I say. "She's not your target audience."

"And who is this handsome man?" The *Glamour* editor is suddenly leaning over me with her hand out.

"Oh! Laura, this is Carter. Carter Hughes, Laura Banks. She's got her first book coming out."

"Oh yeah?" he says. "What's it about?"

"It's about the mistakes people make in relationships."

Carter looks at me and then back at her. "What kind of mistakes?"

"Well, it's never been easier to go on a date than right now, right? And yet, in these turbulent times, it's never been harder to find *real love*. Just like there's junk food, there's junk love. Tantalizing packages that are widely available, but it's ultimately superficial. My book is about how you have to wade through the cookies and potato chips to find the produce aisle, and that's where you'll find a *real* relationship grounded in trust and intimacy."

"In the produce aisle?" he says.

"Exactly. Away from the empty calories."

"So it's a diet book," I explain to Carter. "About relationships."

I am somewhat smiling, but I can't tell if he knows how full of shit I really think she is.

Either way, Laura is delighted. "Exactly! It's about clearing out your cupboards and sweeping your fridge and doing a dating detox not dissimilar to what you'd do to reset your metabolism." She leans into him. "Tell me, Carter. Are you dating anyone?"

"Not anyone in particular, no," he says, looking at me. "But I'd like to be."

"Because you won't get skinny from eating the same old shit!" she yells at him.

He nods. "I'll keep that in mind."

"Alcohol is not a food group. Many men your age don't understand that. Stick to natural sugars. Porn is like chewing gum. All artificial flavor. Trust your gut. Set your own 'best before' date."

A woman at Laura's table is demanding her attention, so she says: "Anyway, Carter, nice to meet you! Life is a feast! Take your place at the table!"

"You've given me a lot to think about. Thank you," he says to her.

I look at him after Laura sits back down. "You're welcome!"

"Jesus," he says. "So when do you get out of here?"

"Hmmm . . . There's a Q&A after this, then a dinner. Rich people pay to host dinner parties for the authors. Mine is at some mansion in Water Mill."

My agent comes over. "Jess, I want to introduce you to

someone." He raises his eyebrows. "She writes for *The New York Review of Books*."

I shrug at Carter. "Gotta go." I leave him standing there. I feel a pang of guilt, but I brush it away. *He's an adult. He can manage.*

"Okay," I say, trailing behind my agent as we cross the tent. "But I'm canceling the Q&A."

"*What?*"

"I'm not doing it. I hate this shit. I'll get up there and talk, but I'm not answering idiotic questions about my characters and how they intersect with my personal life."

He is outraged. "So what are you going to do up there? Wimbledon highlights?"

Two hours later I am sitting at the head of a long table. It is a table next to the pool house, the catering side of some media mogul's compound. The sun has set. Three courses have been served amongst flickering candles. I have been entertaining people all night. I have been talking talking talking, asking questions, making jokes. I've been offered a stay at a house in Spain, if ever I'm in the neighborhood. Some guy wants me to be his doubles partner at his country club in Southampton. Apparently, my agent has told him all about me, boasting about my glory days as a junior tennis player the same way he does my literary stats. There's a mixed doubles tournament this weekend. He'll take care of everything for me. I just have to show up.

"Ah, I only play on grass during the summer," I tell him.

And then, for a brief moment, the residents of my table are occupied, and I can sit back and be quiet. And thank god, because

I am *wiped*, can barely formulate a sentence. But then, as I take a moment to myself, the inevitable happens. I start thinking about Carter. This is followed shortly by a wave of pleasure ricocheting through my body. *Dammit. Why. Why. Why. Why.* I'm not sure if he stayed for the Q&A. I deliberately tried not to look for him in the crowd, not wanting to know, so desperate to focus on the task at hand, to stay in the present.

I take out my phone. But then I put it back down. *No. No. No. No. No. Cut it out. Now. Before this gets any worse.*

A man sits down next to me. He's an editor I met once at an awards dinner at the New School in the Village. He wants to chat about the novel he just finished working on.

"The narrative itself doubles as an anthem of resistance, actually, in many ways, a case against the eradication of our environment," he says. "It's inspired by Orwell and McCarthy, of course, a real literary tapestry. The result is quite extraordinary. Though it raises some dire questions about technology and the direction we are headed in as a species."

"Right."

"The author's style is omnivorous, *jarringly* omnivorous. His writing has an almost cartoonish violence and then a great lyrical beauty all at once."

"Oh yeah?" I say, taking a sip of my ice water to keep myself from falling asleep.

"And it's not about the Egypt that *you* know," he says, shaking his head.

The Egypt that I know? When have we ever spoken about Egypt?

"No. It's about the Egypt of *the senses*, the Egypt of the soul, cut open . . . "

He gets more heated. I start to zone out.

He says: "The editing required so much—the ability to translate verse with a strict meter, a capacity to go from the highest, most literary registers to something that is almost idiomatic. It felt like a watershed moment in my life as an editor."

"Wow. Sounds like a real . . . journey."

"I hope people see how solemn this novel is, that beneath the playful exterior, it is actually a call to action for readers to do all they can to avoid the demonic world it portrays from becoming a reality."

I slyly reach down for my phone. The second the editor gets up, I text Carter:

Do you want to get drunk and go swimming with me?

13

CARTER

I'VE HAD ABOUT ENOUGH. I'M CLOSING this deal.

I wait until I hear her car in her driveway, then I walk to her house. I'm walking, or at least I think I'm walking. I don't feel much like a person, more like a pile of nerve endings that is somehow making its way from one place to another. I don't go into the house, just head straight to the gate, which opens into the backyard.

The gate is tricky, and apparently doesn't respond to throwing your whole body directly into it. Four times. I reach over the top and fiddle with the lock, which doesn't work. It jingles, but doesn't open. I have one remaining option and that is to break it, leaving in my wake a small piece of silver metal, lying on the grass.

"Somebody broke your gate," I say to her, she who is sitting with her legs crossed on a lounge chair in a black bikini. She is drinking a beer.

She laughs and rubs her forehead. "Oh, really? Who was it? That rabbit who is always running in and out of the bushes?" She stands up.

"Could be."

She crosses her backyard to examine the damage. I run my eyes over her whole body, not sure where to look first. I'm taking it all in. I want to touch and lick and I don't know where to begin.

"Carter, what the fuck! The guy who owns this place is going to kill me . . . "

"Has he seen you? You'll be fine."

"You could have just called me . . . I was sitting right here."

She sits back down, hands me a can, and then shifts on her towel so that she is lying down. I sit next to her. I am trying not to ogle her. I am trying to look her in the eye, to pretend like I'm not losing my fucking mind. I have no idea the degree to which I am pulling this off, but I am trying.

I take a long sip and put my hand underneath her thigh and squeeze. I say: "Let's go in the water."

We take our drinks to the edge of the pool. We get in.

Once I get her in the pool, I'm relaxed. The water slows me down, makes me feel in less of a rush. I can take my time. She wants me. I want her. It's no longer a matter of *if*, just when, how, what. A question of strategy.

The water is dark, but there is a circular light at each end of the pool, illuminating our fragmented bodies. Her legs are bent under the water and the only thing I can see clearly is her head and the tops of her shoulders, the straps of her bathing suit tied behind her neck.

We wade around in the water for a while.

"How was your night?" I ask. "Did you sell all your copies?"

"Every last one."

"I bet."

I shake my head. "That *Glamour* chick."

"I know. Believe me, I know."

She goes underwater and swims to the other side of the pool. I watch as her legs go from one end of the pool to the other. She comes up for air, rubs her eyes. She looks even more beautiful coming out of the water, with her hair and eyelashes wet.

"Did you know that there's a blue moon tonight?" I ask her.

She looks up. "*Oh*. Wow," she says. "The moon . . . the stars. You're really pulling out all the stops for me."

"Whatever it takes."

"I had no idea there'd be a blue moon tonight," she says, still looking up.

"That's because you don't live with a psychotic goalie."

"What does it mean? Did he tell you?"

"Of course he told me. He hasn't been able to shut up about it."

"Tell me," she says, softly.

I move my arms across the surface of the water, getting closer to her. "Well, it's very rare."

She takes a step back. "That I knew."

"It can accelerate your response to things. If there's something you've been thinking about doing, now is the time. It means it's time to level up."

I take a step forward.

"Well, isn't that *interesting*."

"Hey, I don't make the rules."

Every time I get close to her, she swims away, goes to the steps of the pool, crosses to the deep end, sips from her beer. It's becoming a ridiculous game of cat and mouse, the underwater version.

Once she stops moving, I position myself right in front of her, at the halfway point of the pool. Our bodies are a foot apart.

I lean into her ear, whisper: "Why are you torturing me?"

Under the water, I hold the sides of her waist with my hands. It feels so good that I almost can't stand it. I touch the back of my hand to her stomach, graze over her belly button. She takes a step back, wriggles my hands off her.

She says: "Because I'm the one with something to lose."

"I have something to lose. You could walk away from this at any time."

"That's not the same thing."

She widens her eyes and then splashes a bunch of water in my face. I go underwater for cover, and by the time I open my eyes again, she's gone.

I see that she's now out of the pool, spreading her towel at the edge of the shallow end. She sits with her legs dangling in the water.

"I don't think we should hang out anymore," she says.

"Fine by me," I reply.

"So this will be our last night?"

"If that's what you want."

Then she lies down on the towel, knees bent, hair strewn behind her across the stone. She turns her head to the side, faces me. She stares up at the sky, and I watch as her knees sway from side to side. I stare at the curve of her hips, the dip of her stomach.

I swim to her. I look up at the blue moon and feel like this night exists outside of time, like there can be no record of these events.

I lean down, kiss the side of her thigh, then keep going until I reach the side of her knee. I play with the side of her bikini bottoms, where the fabric meets her hip bone. She moves slightly to accommodate me. I look at her face. Her eyes are closed. I take two fingers and touch between her legs.

"How long have you been this wet?"

She opens her eyes. "Since I texted you earlier."

"Do you always get this wet when you talk to me?"

"I always get this wet when I talk to you."

I am so hard that I groan as I press, in a state that is almost painful. I groan again as she moans. I press again, and again. Her voice is getting louder. This is the most turned on I've ever been, the sexiest girl I've ever seen in my life.

"Can I take these off?" I say, as I hook my fingers into her bikini. She lifts her butt slightly off the towel, tilting her head back, raising her chin toward the sky. She's running her hand along the side of my body now, across my stomach muscles in a way that is making me *wild*, wild with desire for her.

"Take them off," she says. "Please take them off." I pull them over her ankles and now there is absolutely no stopping me. I shift her body so that I can have both of her legs over my shoulders.

I put my head down and my tongue between her legs and the sound of her breath quickening is the best sound I've ever heard. As I feel her insides with my tongue, her breathing gets louder.

She is playing with my hair, running her fingers along my scalp. She is pushing herself against my mouth and I'm licking her as deeply as I can.

She is arching her back, panting and saying my name, over and over again. *Carter* turns to *harder*. Suddenly, she gasps and I quickly put my fingers inside of her as she bucks up and down and comes against them.

Her body lies flat against the towel. There is a siren in the distance as she catches her breath. I kiss her neck as she comes back down to Earth. My fingers are still inside of her. I am out of breath myself.

The siren gets closer, but because I'm so lust-drunk it doesn't occur to me how rare it is to hear a siren around here.

"Do you smell smoke?" she asks.

"Do I smell smoke?"

She turns to me. "Are they pulling into your driveway?"

I can see red lights closer now, flashing through the bushes. "Shouldn't you go see what's going on?" she says.

"Jessica, my friends could be on fire and I wouldn't go over there right now."

"What about your drugs?"

"Oh, *FUCK*."

The next morning, our car ride to go work out is dead silent. We pull up to the brown-shingled cottage, just off 27, and get out of the car—me in my Nike workout clothes, Harps in some pair of ridiculously short shorts and a tank top, and JT in a headband, wristband, oversized T-shirt, and mesh shorts, looking like he's about to play basketball in the nineties. This class isn't a part of our training regimen, but at some point, we discovered it was a great way to meet women and as far as the workout itself goes—well, it can't hurt. We call it "mobility training," a break from the endless skating drills, the hours of weights at the gym.

On one wall of the cottage, there is a plaque with silver block letters, widely spaced apart: *Tracy Anderson*. The A is not crossed, so it's just an upside-down V. *Groundbreaking*.

"Pass me that water bottle," Harps says as we get out of the car.

"Get it yourself," I reply.

"Geeeeez."

"You could have burned down the house last night," I say. "You guys were acting like fucking amateurs."

JT says: "He's pissed that we blew up his spot last night."

I say: "You had to have fifteen candles lit in your bedroom, Harps? That was pretty fucking stupid."

"It was a blue moon party."

"So?"

"He had to have them lit," JT says. "He did *not* have to forget about them once the girls wanted to go into the hot tub."

"Curtains." Harps shakes his head at the sky. "The curtains were my downfall. I am sorry, man. I regret my actions."

JT says, "I don't regret it. Carter learned a valuable lesson last night: Always screw as if time is of the essence. Because you never know."

"I'm not in the mood for one of your lessons," I say, pulling open the door to the studio.

"Nothing a full-body workout won't cure," JT replies. And I'm hoping he's right. Because my full body feels like shit.

The pop music is already blaring. At this point in the summer, we know almost everybody in there. Harps slept with the girl at the front desk. JT is trying to fuck a blonde in a ponytail and all-white bodysuit who is busy giving specific instructions to another woman about facials.

We put our phones in lockers, then go to opposite corners of the room. It's crowded, a packed class, filled with the sound of women gossiping.

For a hairdresser, he has such a weird hold on her . . .

What kind of surgery is she having again?

You know, people are looking for more personalized gifts these days . . .

The big question is: How much do you need a matching set?

Some are stretching in pastel leggings and neon sneakers, their breasts sticking out of the tops of their sports bras. Some sit on their mats, next to a set of miniature dumbbells.

I roll out my mat. There is one older woman who has been trying to get me to hook up with her all summer. She was married to a banker who turned out to be gay. She got ten million in the divorce. She approaches me, tells me once again about the movie screenings she's doing in her backyard.

"You should come by one night."

"Maybe," I say.

"What night is good for you? We could do tonight! Tomorrow?"

"Oh, I don't know . . ." I look around, over at the door,

where I see Charlotte come in. She is wearing pink leggings with a pink sports bra, her neck covered in gold and diamond necklaces. She has a lace scrunchie around her wrist.

The class is about to start. I watch her face as it dawns on her that there is only one spot available, and it is next to me. She gets closer, gives me a steely look and then goes about setting up her flower-covered mat, positioning her phone to take a video. She is annoyed, but she seems to brush it off. She squints at the mirror, purses her lips. The show must go on.

A girl comes up to her to compliment her hair tie, whispering: "That is *so* cute!"

She whispers back: "So cute, right? I got it at a lace store in *Venezia*. I was in this little lace village. All Edwardian lace. It was a dream. Literally my heaven."

I can feel my muscles tense at the sound of their voices. *So cute, right?*

The class begins. We are on all fours and kicking our legs up into the air. We are balancing on the mat with our hands and swinging our legs from side to side.

Everyone's arms are flailing around. Every time I raise my arms, it's hard not to hit Charlotte's. I have to deliberately avoid her arms, which is hard to do while keeping up with the moves.

"Do you mind?" she says, when my arm collides with hers for the fourth time.

"I do, actually."

Don't get into it with her. It's not worth it. I inhale to the count of four, hold for four, exhale for six.

She goes over to her phone, stops the video. She repositions herself so that she can start a new video, smoothing her hair and tilting her head from side to side to examine herself from different angles.

"You're not supposed to have your phone," I say. "This is a workout class." She pretends not to hear me. Our arms collide again.

"You gotta move over!" I say.

She sighs, goes up to the front of the class, whispers something in Tracy's ear. Tracy looks at me. I clench my fists for ten seconds and then release them. *Challenge negative thoughts. Reframe from a different perspective. Accept the imperfections of others and yourself.* I am trying, but nothing matters besides the monstrousness of this girl. She should get what she deserves.

Charlotte returns to her mat. I stare her down.

"Fucking tattletale," I say to her.

"If you don't stop *harassing* me . . ."

"What are you going to do? Tell all your followers?"

"At least I *have* followers."

"Yeah, you have followers all right, and not much else."

She looks taken aback. Her eyes well up with tears. She turns away from me and stares at Tracy, tries to get back to the routine, but she's moving slowly. She plays with her necklaces, fixes her ponytail.

She turns to me and says, loudly: "You don't belong here."

Tracy stops the music. All the women are staring at us.

"Oh yeah? Well, I was so uninterested in you the other night that I spent the entire time staring at the girl behind you. Why don't you spend a little *more* money on your appearance? Then maybe nobody will notice you're completely devoid of personality. Here's hoping!"

She starts to cry and rolls up her mat. She walks away.

"Fuck you, Carter!" she yells, from across the room, and then swings open the door. Everyone in the class is staring at me.

"She's the worst," I say. "Fuck her."

14

JESSICA

I'M IN A KIND OF PAIN I don't recognize. I'm not eating or sleeping much, just sitting with a massive stomachache that I'm trying to decode like a riddle. I mentally sift through my Rolodex of emotions. *Shock? Guilt? Regret? Sadness?* Nothing seems right. Eventually, I decide that it's all those things, the low after a high. What goes up must come down. I'm forcing myself to cry every now and then because that's more recognizable to me. It's something I've experienced before. Crying feels like the pain might be leaking out, a little bit.

I call Alejandro ten times a day. I am nice, doting. If he doesn't pick up, I am fearing for my life.

There is no getting away from it now, no sugarcoating the truth. I am selfish. I am impulsive. I am bad. There were options, and I chose the worst one, the one that gives in the most to my rotten instincts. The devil on my shoulder didn't even have to fight this time. And now I'm in pain. Big surprise.

I wish, more than anything else, that I were better. And all I can do, in my darkest moments, is write it down, to use later, to offer it up to anyone else who wishes they were better too.

For the next few days, I focus on writing, on turning pain into pages. I stay away from my phone. I don't text Carter, and thankfully he doesn't text me either. I channel all my emotions into something that my characters experience in an entirely different situation. I start to feel better, like the cobwebs are clearing. And then he texts me.

Going for dinner in Sag Harbor tonight with JT and Harps. Want to come?

I slide my phone across the room. I tell myself: *Just say no. That's it. Time's up. Your body has to listen to your brain now.* What I realize over the next few hours is that I can hold off on responding. I can pretend I don't care. But I can't wipe the stupid smile off my face.

And then it dawns on me. *What the fuck is wrong with you? You're falling for this?* Here's the thing about guys like Carter: You don't mean anything to them. Oh, it certainly seems like it. Many skilled performances have been cobbled together to get to this point. But you can be easily replaced. It seems like you can't, because that's how they've gotten you in the first place. But it's an act. A very charming little act. And at age thirty-five, I am in the fortunate position of having seen this play before.

My plan going forward is to shut it down, emotionally. The barriers are up. And the good news is, now I won't get hurt, and now I can go to dinner. I gave in once. I won't do it again. Not in public. Not in front of his friends. It's not really my strong suit, this shutting down of the system, giving placid answers, not really saying how I feel. But I can't be myself anymore. That is the only way to get out of this alive. From now on, I'm going to be Good Jessica. Good Jessica prioritizes her family. Good Jessica eats vegetables. Good Jessica gives short answers. Good Jessica says things like, *What's your favorite season? Mine's spring!*

Unfortunately, I'm not an idiot. And I realize that what I'm doing is sort of like eating an entire pizza at 3 A.M. and then having a lot of lettuce the next day. But I'm going to do it anyway. What choice do I have? I can't turn back time. I can only learn from my mistakes and try to be better. *Next time, when presented with a hot neighbor who wants to fuck you in your backyard: Don't.*

I text him back: *Maybe. What time?*

We can pick you up around 7?

I'll meet you there. I'll stop by after a party I have in East.

Like hell I'm going to let him think I'm sitting around waiting for this dinner like it's the event of the season. His dinner is merely a stop along the way amongst a myriad of imaginary plans I have that evening. As of now, I don't have plans in East Hampton, but in about twenty minutes, I will.

On the car ride into Sag, I call Alejandro and tell him all about the dinner and feel like I am talking to another adult about children.

I get off the phone and focus on parking. I am a little late, as my imaginary-turned-real event ran long, as those tend to do. Also, it's taken me ten minutes to park.

They are seated outside on the patio at an Italian restaurant called Tutto Il Giorno. The patio is filled with potted green plants on a pebble floor, white tables with white umbrellas overhead. Each chair has a white blanket covering the back of the chair. It is meant to have a rustic Italian vibe, but it is way overdone, with so many blankets and white pillows and potted plants that there is nothing rustic about it. The blankets seem excessive. It is probably the warmest night of the summer.

Carter seems a little off from the moment I get there, like something is bothering him. He answers questions brusquely, flings insults about the other diners for no reason.

As we eat, I focus on JT and Harps, ask them questions, prying for information for my book. They are talking about past hookups. They are explaining what they do if they wake up with a girl but want her to leave.

Harps says: "In college I used to pretend I had an early morning job at the library, and then I would leave to go to the job, and she'd leave with me, and then I'd hide behind a wall until she was out of sight. Then I went back to my room."

I think it over. "It's pretty good. It's pretty good. Because you can't just kick her out. But don't you feel bad for lying?"

"No. Girls have plenty of schemes. Do you know how many earrings have been 'accidentally' left at my place?"

"But that's not really the same," I say. "That's because she likes you! You're scheming to get rid of her."

"I don't see the difference," he says.

"Trust me. There's a difference."

As we're talking, Carter is quiet, typing on his phone. My bag is on the ground next to me and I can see my phone lighting up with texts. I look across the table. He stares at me. I look down at my plate. I start to feel a bit unsteady, then good, so good, and then unsteady again. What is he writing? I'm tempted to check my phone. *No. No. No. Why?*

With one hand, I look at my phone under the table, but I don't look directly at it because I'm too afraid of what's there. I read his text with my eyes out of focus. All I can see are a few words:

I want to climb under the table and eat your . . .

Suddenly, my body is flooded with feeling. I take a long sip of my wine. And then another. I grip my wine glass, hard. I want to get up and walk away, to just shake this feeling out of me, but I don't. I can't. I'm frozen in place. I give him a dark look, put my phone on silent, and then shove it back in my bag, making sure to flip it so that I can't see the front. I order another glass of wine.

"Tell her what you did to Charlotte at Tracy's," JT says, then turns to me when Carter is silent. JT laughs. "He told her that he was staring at you the whole time he was hanging out with her, and she cried and left."

"*What?*" I look at Carter. "Why'd you do that?"

Carter says: "She deserved it."

"Why? What did she do?"

He pauses. "She put her mat too close to mine."

I screw up my face. "That's unnecessarily mean."

"It's a workout class," he says. "I'm a professional athlete."

"Oh, *get over yourself*," I reply, laughing, and he looks sullen.

JT changes the subject. Harps suggests a game where we look at all the other tables in the restaurant and decide what their deal is. *Are they coworkers? A third date? Is it a family? Is it a man with a much younger girlfriend or is that his daughter?*

A man comes up to JT. He is red-faced and wearing a navy

sweater, a plaid shirt visible at the collar. He leans over JT's chair and says: "I'm surprised you would show your face here."

A bad feeling comes over me. JT looks up at him. "Excuse me? Do I know you?"

"You do," the guy says. "You slept with my wife."

JT swallows. "You're going to have to be more specific."

The guy almost smiles but doesn't. He responds: "I chased you out of my house with a kitchen knife."

"Ohh," JT says. "Sorry. I didn't recognize you without your golf clothes on."

He looks taken aback. "You'd better hope you don't run into me again."

JT scoffs. "Oh yeah? Or what?"

Carter stands up.

The guy nods to himself. "You know, you *really* shouldn't fuck around with people in the Hamptons . . . you never know who you're talking to, or who they might be friends with."

Carter says, "We don't give a fuck about your friends."

The guy laughs. "I am really going to enjoy ruining your lives. I mean it. I am going to *savor* the moment when I make that call."

I watch as Carter pushes him into a table of women, who all gasp. Plates and glasses crash to the floor. The rest of the diners are horrified. The man gets up off the floor and examines himself for damage.

It is silent. Everyone is staring. People don't know what to do. *I* don't know what to do.

A man in a linen shirt, presumably the manager, comes up to our table. He looks at Carter. "Hey, man, I have to ask you to leave."

I head to my car, walking at a brisk pace, and Carter follows me. I stop and turn toward him, but I don't know what to say. So we stand there, on the street, each waiting for the other to say something. I can feel drops of sweat gathering in my eyebrows. The heat is like a weight in the air, a pressure on my skin. There is a low rumble of thunder in the distance, the occasional flash of lightning.

"What *was* that?" I ask.

"What do you mean?"

"You threw that guy across the room!"

"I just pushed him a little."

"That wasn't a normal push. It wasn't even that big of a deal. It wasn't even your fight!"

"It *was* my fight. JT is one of my closest friends. If somebody threatens him, I'll kill them. He's lucky. He got off easy."

"What about the fact that JT slept with his *wife*? Do the laws of matrimony mean nothing to you?"

He laughs, loudly. "That's rich, coming from you."

"And why would you say that to that girl, Charlotte? You made her cry? Don't you feel bad? Don't you feel *anything*?"

"I don't think that's any of your business," he says. "But everything is your business, right?"

"What's *that* mean?"

"It means we're all such interesting material to you. You're using all of us for your own selfish gain. Do you even love your family or do you just need them for the jokes?"

I am stunned. All I can do is repeat his words back to him, slowly. "*Do I even love my family?*"

He goes on: "How much material have you gotten out of

us? Out of me? How much material are you getting right now? Are you recording this conversation? If not, you'd better write it down! You might forget!"

"You know what? Congratulations on being able to correctly identify everyone else's vulnerabilities. I hope nobody ever turns the tables on you." I am shaking, with tears in my eyes, as I take my car keys out of my bag. "I *never* want to see you again."

"I'll drive you," he says.

"I can drive myself."

"You've been drinking."

"So have you!"

"Yeah, but I can handle myself. And you can barely drive sober."

I hit the button that unlocks my car.

"Give me the keys," he says.

"*No.* Why don't you go find a *model* or an *influencer* or a *billionaire's daughter* and leave me the fuck alone."

"Oh my god. You're exhausting."

"*Am I?* Or are you just not used to expending mental energy for more than twenty minutes at a time?" I put my hands on my hips. "Is your brain okay? Do you need me to take you to the fucking hospital?"

He comes up to me and tries to pry the keys from my hands. I shove him, then whack his arm with my fist. He holds my wrist so that I don't whack him again, then shakes it so that the keys fall out of my hand and onto the pavement, and he grabs them. I grip his arm, try to tear them out of his hands, and we continue to battle over my car keys on the streets of Sag Harbor, outside of Tutto Il Giorno, right next to a lovely gathering of potted plants.

A police officer comes up to us. "Excuse me, Miss? Is this man bothering you?"

"Now that you mention it, he is," I say to him.

"*Jessica,*" Carter says sternly.

I smile. "I'm just kidding. We're messing around. He's fine. He's famous!" I shrug. "It's the Hamptons!"

"She has a weird sense of humor," Carter explains.

We stand there silently as the officer moves along. He looks back at us several times from down the block. I smile. Wave. Smile. *Nothing to see here.*

I feel drops of rain on my arm, a few falling on my head. I look up.

"Oh, for fuck's sake," I say. "Fine. Just drive me home."

We get in the car and sit in silence. It feels like a furnace, but I can't open the windows because the rain is coming down hard against them. I turn on the air conditioning. I catch my breath. I can feel myself calming down. We drive by the boats in the harbor, rows and rows of sailboats, all rocking in the warm wind.

The lightning is visible in flashes overhead and there are bolts in the distance. I can feel my anger start to dissipate. Unfortunately, I can also feel my anger slowly turning into something else. Pleasure. Intense waves of it. So intense that it feels like a problem. So intense that I feel like I might not be okay.

FUCK. WHY?

I look over at him. He looks increasingly agitated, keeps glancing over at my legs, tightens his grip on the steering wheel. I am fidgeting, touching my face a lot, nervously playing with my hair. I uncross and recross my legs.

The sky continues to flicker, bright white among dark clouds, the clouds turning on and off as if lit up by lamps. The lightning is mimicking the flashes of heat inside of my body. He's making little noises. I'm not even sure what they are. He sighs, appears to be having a silent argument with himself.

I turn up the air conditioning. *It's okay. You're fine. It'll pass. Just ride it out. Think of something else. Think of your kids. Your family. Pull it together for the next twenty minutes, and then you can break down at home, alone.* But nothing works. All roads lead back to this. My mind will not leave this place. It is stuck like glue to the present moment.

The waves start hitting me harder. They last longer. He starts drumming the steering wheel with his right hand, tapping it with his fingers at a constant pace. He turns the music on. I glance at the dashboard.

"#41"—*Live at Luther College, Dave Matthews & Tim Reynolds* comes droning out of the car speakers. I sigh. *You've got to be kidding me.*

"I love this song," he says.

"So do I," I reply.

How does he even know this song? Isn't he too young?

I take my sweater off, hold it in a ball in my hands.

My body is hot and tingly. My heart is behaving erratically. I keep looking over at him, for a few seconds at a time, because my only solace is that we're in this together. He keeps looking over at me, but we never look at the same time, until he stops at a red light, and then we do.

He touches my knee. He knows. I know.

He makes a sharp turn onto North Sea Road. It is a road that winds uphill, with small houses, erratically spaced apart. If you look carefully, between the wild, untamed shrubbery, you can see glimpses of water.

It is quiet. We can hear only the music, our breathing, and the rain. He drives to the end of the street, which is a dead end. I can see a small path that leads to the water. He puts the car in park, gets out, into the rain. I hear my trunk open, him rummaging around, and then the sound of the trunk slamming shut. I sit there feeling my heart gallop. He appears at my door and opens it. He has a manic look in his eyes, peering down at me with a beach towel in his hands, his hair and shirt already soaked. I stare at his body, the way his wet shirt hangs against his shoulders and stomach muscles. We are just two bodies now, and they have to get as close together as possible.

I've lost. I've already lost.

I climb out of the car and take his hand, follow him through a small patch of woods. Beyond the woods, there is grass, sand, the bay. I am soaked by the time we reach the sand. With one hand, he spreads the towel on the sand. I try to let go of his hand, so that it's easier for him to spread the towel, but he won't let me.

"Take off your clothes," I say, as I take off my top, and drop down to my knees.

I sit in a white skirt and pink bra, facing him. He takes off his shirt, then stands there, frozen.

I laugh a little. "You're shy, suddenly?" I say, and then unbutton his shorts. I take them off, along with his underwear.

I run my fingers along his dick and then go toward it with my mouth. He's so ready for me. I look up at him.

"I need to kiss you first," he says, and then leans down.

We kiss and his mouth feels so good, but I need more. He stands up straight.

I put his dick in my mouth. He looks up at the sky.

"I can't. You can't do that. You're going to make me come. I need to be inside of you."

"Lie down," I say, and peel off my skirt and underwear, unhook my bra. My nipples are hard from the rain. I straddle him, moving involuntarily. I lean forward and he puts one nipple into his mouth. I arch my back as he uses one of his hands to play with my clit. I am talking, involuntarily.

Oh, your dick is so big.

It feels so good.

Oh, fuck, that feels amazing.

I'm gonna come.

I rock back and forth. He is squeezing my ass, hard, spreading me wide open.

Suddenly, I am coming, gasping for air. I let out a cry, my mouth wide, and then lurch forward, collapse onto him, face buried in the towel. He holds onto me as I breathe.

I feel him push up into me, hear his breathing get heavier, too, into my neck. He grips me as he sharply exhales. With his chest against mine, I can feel his heart beating fast. Mine is right there too.

We shift so that we are both on our sides, our arms still wrapped around each other. He is watching me, I can tell, and it makes me self-conscious, so I throw my arm across my face, cover my eyes with the inside of my elbow, and start to laugh. He laughs at me, and then we are just two bodies, laughing.

15

CARTER

I'VE BEEN THINKING ABOUT IT FOR weeks. It's been haunting me. The ten 400 drill. It's so grueling. Ten 400-meter sprints around a track.

I'm riding such a high that I want to get after it now. I want to get it done. I'm the one to suggest it. I get everyone in the car and drive us to the nearest track.

At the track, I look up at the scoreboard: *Southampton High School* in white and maroon lettering, looming over the football field. The track surrounds the field.

The first lap is easy. We look at our watches, wait for our heart rates to go below 130 BPM. They come down quick. Then we start on the second.

I'm killing JT and Harps.

"You're feeling awfully good about yourself today," JT says, taking a sip of water. "Is this the Jessica effect?"

"No," I say. "Last month of training. That's all."

I will admit nothing.

After the fourth lap, Harps is gasping for wind. By the fifth, JT starts to spit as we run, sucking snot in through his nose and mouth, basically falling apart.

Shirts come off. We're grabbing towels. The time it takes to get our heart rates down gets longer.

"Holy fuck," I hear JT say after the sixth lap. He's breathing through his mouth. He's done.

We're pouring bottles of water on ourselves. Sweat is rolling down my forehead, the salt burning my eyes. We've got sweat bands on our wrists, and we're using them, but with all the sweat, it's still like running blind.

We are trying to push each other. We are shouting things like:

You have to dig deep in overtime!

Do you want to be a great third-period player? DO YOU?

By the eighth lap, we lose the ability to form words. JT quits altogether. On lap nine, Harps is dry heaving.

It's like a tidal wave. I feel like I'm under ten feet of water, which turns into twenty. The mountain is getting higher and higher. I want to finish faster than I started, but it's hard.

Once we're done, I lie on the grass next to the track.

My phone rings from an unknown number. *Oyster Bay*. I pick up.

"Carter Hughes?"

"Yeah?"

"This is Mr. Howard's executive assistant. He'd like to speak to you."

I clear my throat. "Okay."

I expect to hear him take the phone, but instead she says: "There's a helicopter waiting for you at the East Hampton airport. It'll be there for the next hour."

"For me? Now?"

"Yes, Mr. Hughes."

"Can I ask what this is regarding?"

"I'm sorry?"

"Do you know what this is about?"

"I'm not sure what you mean."

I pause. "Is there any information you can give me?"

"We'll see you soon."

"Wait. Hold on."

I hear the line go dead. *FUCK. What is this?*

"Who was that?" JT says.

"Nobody," I say.

"Sounded like somebody," says Harps.

They're pretty out of it, too tired to ask me anything else. I say: "Let's go."

I don't call my agent. I don't tell my friends. Nobody needs to know that Ryan Howard, owner of the Rangers, has called me for an impromptu meeting. But they can see something is off. I've raced home, showered, and now I'm headed to "see a movie" in the middle of the day by myself. Not suspicious at all.

I drive to East Hampton and turn when I see the sign for the East Hampton Airport. I walk onto the tarmac. There is a whole crew that greets me there, in navy polo shirts and pressed khakis. They look like they're about to welcome me onto a yacht. I can't believe this type of thing exists in real life. *Why is this being sent for me?*

On board, there are two pilots. A pretty flight attendant sits across from me. We take off. It's an incredible ride, flying over the edge of Long Island, following the coast and endless beaches. Unfortunately, I can't really take it in. I don't understand where I'm going or why. A half hour later, we land on a helipad with the MSG logo on it.

They take me to the house in a golf cart.

The house is a large brick compound, with a long stone wall running along the edge of it. Inside, it is empty, but for the one woman showing me where to go.

We pass through a room with red walls, red chairs, and a massive gold chandelier. Another room is pale blue, with a cabinet full of teacups and a dresser displaying pottery and porcelain plates. There is a hallway filled with oil paintings and sculptures, a library with tiers and tiers of bookcases, a large fireplace adorned with marble busts of men. It looks like an Italian museum, like the Vatican, or a scene out of *The Godfather*. The ceilings are painted. The staircase is made of dark wood that is carved into leaves and flowers and the face of a lion.

She instructs me to go outside, which is where I find Howard, sitting on his expansive patio with his feet on the table and a newspaper in his hand. The patio is enclosed by stone pillars, and beyond that is a formal garden, roses and marble benches, hedges shaped like elephants, a velvet lawn.

He barely looks up at me. "Carter Hughes," he mumbles. "How are you?"

"I'm good, boss. How are you?"

"How are you feeling? How's your weight?"

"Great."

"Do you feel strong? Ready for the season?"

I sit across from him and nod.

"How about something to drink? Water? Whiskey? A protein shake?"

I smile. "Is this a test?"

He juts out his lower lip. "I don't have time for tests."

I ask for water. I see no people anywhere, yet somehow the glass appears within no time.

He has a cigar in his mouth but it's not lit. He just chews. He appears to be doing a crossword. He still isn't looking at me.

"So you're out in the Hamptons this summer."

"I am," is all I can muster.

"Heard you bumped into a friend of mine in Sag Harbor . . ." He keeps talking to what seems like himself. "Heard you bumped into him quite hard . . . You don't have many friends in business . . . The king has many servants, but not a lot of friends."

Is he the king and I'm the servant? Or am I the king? And who's the friend?

I am silent.

"Look. I like you. Not everyone does. But I do. So I'm going to be honest with you." He looks at me directly for the first time. "It seems like you're making a lot of assumptions."

"How do you mean?"

"Well, you think you can throw somebody across a restaurant. You think you can fuck other people's wives. And everything will remain in place." He pauses.

I take a sip of water. *Other people's wives.* I'm not sure whether he's talking about JT or Jessica.

"And the thing I love about hockey . . . the thing that *you* probably love about hockey . . . is that it's always moving. A play in any other sport doesn't move nearly as fast. The whole sport is on wheels. When I look at you, I see a guy who has crossed the line many times. I see a guy who thinks that everything he has now will always be his, no matter what."

I feel a tightness in my throat.

He asks: "Are you familiar with Hindu philosophy?"

"Not really."

"The Bhagavad Gita. Three-thousand-year-old Hindu scripture. Gotta be good, right?"

"I guess."

"There's a part in there I particularly like. It says: You're entitled to your labor. You're not entitled to the fruits of your labor."

I stare at him.

"That's it," he says, looking up at me briefly. "You can go now."

I pause, then stand.

As I walk out the door, I can hear him mumble: "The UV index is going to be high for the next few days. I would wear sunscreen if I were you."

"Okay, boss. Thanks again."

I leave in a fog. I am being ushered out of a house in Oyster Bay. I am headed back to the Hamptons, to a house that isn't mine. There is no anchor in any of this, no way to see the center of gravity. I feel like somebody has taken the ground from beneath me, and all that's left is for me to float in space, and for some odd reason, in a helicopter.

When I get home, I don't talk to anyone. JT and Harps go out. I don't go. I need to stay home, where I'm surrounded by four walls, by my belongings, by things that feel real, that are certainly mine.

I shoot pucks and then go in the pool. When I go back into the house, I hear the door open. It's JT's sister, Jill.

"Where are the guys?" she asks me. "I have their paychecks." She puts two envelopes on the kitchen table. She touches her hand to her forehead. She is wearing baggy sweatpants and a cropped T-shirt. She looks exhausted.

"They went to a vineyard," I say. "And then they're going to some beach barbecue/bonfire/clambake."

She groans. "I have *had* it with the Hamptons," she says, and plops down on our coach. She looks at me in a daze. "Do you have something that we can smoke?"

"I do," I say. I go about preparing a joint.

She takes a couple of hits and rambles in between. She doesn't stop talking, just unloads a series of long monologues on me.

"Everyone is *white* and *rich* and nobody has any concept of what life is like outside of this. It's like this weird little alternate universe where everyone can ride around in their giant fucking SUVs and feel entitled. *Ohhhh those flowers are too big! It looks like Bloomingdale's! Do you have a more bohemian tablecloth? Bohemian, but sophisticated bohemian. I don't want it to feel like Vermont! The canapés should be bite-sized! Otherwise, it's just grotesque!* And the worst part is not the excess or the waste, which is considerable, it's the fact that they don't even realize how abnormally privileged they are. They think that people are just irrationally jealous of them and how dare they sometimes show it. This is a legitimate woe of theirs."

"Well, at least you haven't become bitter or anything."

She narrows her eyes at me. "I will tell you this. I am not the same person that I was at the beginning of the summer, Carter," she says, shaking her head. "And you know what? I'm okay with that."

At some point, I am just high enough to come clean about everything. I tell her about the incident at Tutto, about my meeting with Howard. After I'm done, she is quiet, contemplative.

"How bad is this?" I ask.

"You are such fucking idiots," she says.

"Okay. Fine. But worst-case scenario, what can this guy do to us?"

"Well, JT could get his contract ripped up. That would take about eight seconds out of his day. And you could be traded to Winnipeg for spare parts."

"He wouldn't do that."

She laughs. "Oh, he wouldn't? You're dealing with the owner of the Rangers, the Knicks, Madison Square Garden. He doesn't just own the teams. He owns the arena, the network. And he's the only owner in all of sports that has a setup like this, across all leagues. He can sway political elections. Nobody has more juice than Ryan Howard."

"He wanted me on his team. I could have gone anywhere."

"*Please.* You think he gives a shit about you? His job is to manage his assets, and when he feels like an asset is no longer working for him, he gets rid of it."

16

JESSICA

IT KEEPS COMING BACK TO ME in flashes.

I am driving, the sun beating down on my windshield. I am focused on not dying in a horrific car crash. *Flash* of the bay at night, pitch black, his face and hair in the rain.

I smile at the cashier at the Golden Pear. "Hi, can I please have a . . . " *Flash* of his naked body, him saying: *I need to kiss you first.*

I walk across a parking lot with a coffee in my hand. *Flash* of my body falling forward into his.

I am talking on the phone with Alejandro, staying in the moment, very carefully staying in the moment, and then, there is a lull. *Flash* of my voice saying: *Oh, fuck, that feels amazing.*

I wake up from dreams about Carter and find myself reaching for the nearest notebook, which turns out to be a notebook that I bought for my daughter. It's pink with a picture of Hello Kitty on the cover. It says *Stay Cute*. I am hesitant to use it. I am mortified, actually. But I don't want to be on my phone or computer in the middle of the night and it's got to land somewhere. So I reach for it and write down the dirtiest things I've ever written. Avert your eyes, Hello Kitty.

I wake up the next morning and open the notebook, to see if there's anything in there I can use for my novel. It's like surveying the wreckage after a hurricane. I examine my scribbles on the page, the flying debris that's landed.

I've never experienced anything like this before, not to this degree. My first thought is that maybe I'm in the throes of some kind of deep lust that only hits women during their thirties. I google it. Nothing. My second thought is that maybe I'm a sex addict. I google it, just to be sure, just to rule it out. But I don't seem to qualify. Because it's not about sex with anyone. It's about him, specifically.

I tell the Internet: *But the cravings don't get put out!* They only seem to get worse. I can't think straight, can't find a way to stay trapped in the guilt I should feel because I'm simply overpowered. Or I'm a sex addict. Time will tell.

All day, I am fighting an internal battle over whether to text him.

Don't do it.

Don't do it.

DON'T.

But as soon as the sun goes down, I take my phone and go to his name and start typing: *Come over?*

And now I wait for his response in *agony*. WHY *did you do this to yourself, Jessica?* WHY? I'm in such a state that I say this, out loud, to myself, while pacing around my house. *You could have had a pleasant evening!* But I don't want a pleasant evening. If I know one thing about myself, it is this: Jessica does not want a pleasant evening. She wants angst and chaos, and she won't stop until she gets it.

My phone beeps. I look at the screen. *Carter Hughes.* I click on his name. It says:

YES.

Well, I guess that makes two of us.

I look in the mirror and try to decide if what I'm wearing is sexy. It's exactly what I've been wearing all afternoon to lounge around the house—white pajama shorts with tiny yellow flowers on them and a white T-shirt that's slightly see-through, no bra. I briefly consider putting on lingerie or something more exotic, but the shorts barely cover my butt and when I stand straight, you can see a strip of my stomach, so I decide to go with it. A real "come as you are" type of policy.

He knocks. My heart takes off.

I open the door, and he lifts me up and takes me to the staircase, places me down on the steps, kisses me with the door wide open. We are ravenous for each other, as the night air blows through the whole house. I almost fuck him right there on the stairs with the door open.

I am pulling him toward me with the back of his head, with his T-shirt, with his waist. I hear a car whizz by and it startles me. I move my lips and body to the side. We are both breathing deeply like we've been submerged under water.

"Holy shit," he says.

"Let's go upstairs."

I close and lock the front door. I follow him upstairs. He doesn't look around at anything. He walks around like he's been here a hundred times before.

My bedroom is dimly lit, just one small lamp is on, on my desk. He goes to turn it off.

"Leave it on," I say. "I want to see you."

He turns and kisses me. "I want to see you too," he says, running his hands along my hips and thighs.

The window is cracked slightly open and it's chilly. I get into bed and pull the covers over me, taking my clothes off under the comforter, and throwing them on the floor. He takes his clothes off across the room and gets into bed, positions himself on top of me.

We are kissing naked, and it's so satisfying to finally have his body all to myself, in my bed. My legs are wrapped around him. I take his dick and use it to play with myself. I'm so wet for him, always.

"Go slow," I say. "I want to feel it. I want to feel everything."

"I will," he says. And then I kiss him until the feeling is too good, until I can't kiss anymore. I have to moan instead. We do this for a while, totally consumed by the feeling, incapable of making any sort of slight change in movement. He goes slow.

"Do you want to stay like this?" he asks.

"Sure," I say.

"Really?"

"No."

I wiggle away from him and turn over onto my stomach and he slips inside of me. He touches my butt, my hips, my stomach, and I'm face down on my forearms.

He's going faster now, grazing my nipples, touching my back. I'm pushing back into him. I can feel myself getting close.

Don't stop. Keep doing that. Don't stop.

I just keep saying it, my mouth in the comforter. He touches my clit.

I groan. *Harder. Faster. Harder.* I gasp. He presses down on me as I come.

I breathe heavily into the comforter, and I can feel him gathering my hair and putting it to one side of my neck, kissing the other side. He grabs my ass and starts going hard again. I feel like he's deeper inside of me somehow and like I'm enjoying my orgasm all over again, like it might happen again. I feel split open and raw, like he's hitting every nerve ending that I have in my body. He's about to come, and I love the feeling of him coming, of him losing control. I love what my body is doing to him, that for those few seconds, he is mine, all mine, and nothing and nobody can take him away from me.

Soon, his body collapses onto mine, and his arms are around me. We roll to the side, lie next to each other in bed, the covers haphazardly strewn across our bodies.

"You have nice feet," he says, holding onto my foot. "I don't typically like feet, but yours are nice. My feet are so flat from being in skates."

"No problem here," I say, pulling my toes back, showcasing my arch.

"My god. How do you even walk? Your feet only hit the ground in two places."

"I get by," I reply. "Oh! You want to see something?"

"Okay . . . "

I pull the covers down so that he can see my stomach. "I've been swimming so much that . . . look! Parentheses!" I touch a slight indentation on one side of my stomach, then the other.

"You mean ab muscles?"

"I've never had them so visible before! It's very exciting."

"Yeah . . . it looks nice," he says, and then traces his finger along the line. "Parentheses . . . "

"That's what they look like to me."

"You're such a nerd."

We decide to get dressed and go downstairs to the kitchen to find something to eat. He puts his phone on the kitchen table.

"I made a playlist," he said.

I laugh. "You did? *You're* such a nerd."

"Yup. Six songs. Thirty minutes apiece. Three uninterrupted hours of Phish."

"This relationship is over."

The music starts. "Settle in," he says, and opens my fridge. "What do you have?"

I look around. It is a paltry selection. "Eggs . . . bread."

"Egg in a hole it is."

I hand him a frying pan. "Isn't it called something else? Like . . . egg in a nest?"

"No. Just . . . egg in a hole."

"But 'nest' is so much more romantic."

I sit at the kitchen table.

"There's no nest!" he says, looking back at me. "It's just a hole."

He removes a shot glass from the cabinet and carves holes into two pieces of bread.

"I think it's a nest." I can hear sizzling butter.

"*Eggs in a nest?* I've never heard that before in my life."

"Maybe you're not running in the right breakfast circles."

"That's a low blow."

"'Nest' is a much nicer word. It implies a home for the egg, which implies shelter. A hole is a black hole, something you fall through. It's bleak."

He rolls his eyes. "The world is full of dark mysteries. Best to realize that at breakfast. It's a hole."

I get up, stand next to him and get in his face. "I will not concede this point and nothing you say or do will make me."

"Then I'm sorry, but we're at an impasse."

"Apparently."

"Kiss and make up?"

I move in closer to him, and we kiss. He turns and as we keep kissing, he presses me against the oven, reaches behind me to turn off the burner.

We eat sitting on the floor in the living room, with our plates on a low table that contains coffee table books and a few of my children's toys. When we finish eating, he surveys the packs of card games on the table.

"Up for a game of Crazy Eights?" he asks.

I look through the pile. "How about a more sophisticated game? Like Slap Jack."

I split the cards into two piles. We play Slap Jack, then Old Maid, then Crazy Eights, then Go Fish. There is a lot of hand slapping on the table. Cursing. Yelling.

This is the most out of hand Old Maid has ever gotten!

A Crazy Eight is not carte blanche to do whatever you want!

What's unfair? How can it possibly be unfair? Those are the rules!

HEY! You can't slap just to slap!

At some point, the cards are all over the floor, because we've thrown them at each other. He says: "I'd like to declare a truce and go outside and teach you how to roll a joint."

I laugh. "Do you have the necessary ingredients here to do that?"

"Always."

We go out to the patio. I shiver and rub my arms, and he takes off his sweatshirt, hands it to me. I struggle to roll the paper properly. He gets frustrated and does it himself. I take one hit and blow the smoke out of my mouth.

"Look at you. You didn't even cough."

I shrug. "I'm a game-time player."

"Well, your pregame is atrocious. You don't ever smoke?" he asks me.

"Not really. I used to, when I was your age, but now I just drink and microdose Xanax, like an adult."

"Are you kidding?"

"I wish I were."

"Why Xanax?"

I laugh, crossing my legs and leaning back into the cushy patio chair. "Because I'm prone to panic attacks, and when I have one, Xanax makes it stop."

"I've never had a panic attack."

"Eh, it's not that big of a deal. You just feel like you can't breathe and like you're going to die for a few minutes, but then it passes."

"That sounds like a big deal."

"I started having them senior year of college, but more often when I was in my twenties. I'm not the most level-headed person you've met," I say, laughing. "I run on adrenaline and bad decisions. Like I have a list, in my head, of all the people who have said 'no' to me. I think about them almost every day."

"I call it a revenge bin."

"My list is long."

"My revenge bin is full."

I laugh. "You need a lot of mental fortitude to withstand heaps of rejection as a writer! Not to mention play a five-hour tennis match against a Russian girl twice your size whose father is ready to kill her if she loses. I'm sure you've needed it too. Sometimes I use that power for good, and sometimes I use it to destroy myself."

"It has to have somewhere to go," he says.

"A safe landing space."

We start talking about our childhoods, adolescence, college.

"I was a theater major, you know," he says.

"Were you? I gotta tell you . . . I can't picture you doing theater."

"I can act."

I stare at him. "Prove it."

"I will! I'll do a fucking *Shakespeare* monologue for you."

I make a sweeping motion with my hand. "I'm waiting."

Before I know it, the sky is beginning to brighten, and we're on our second round of our sixth Phish song and he's doing *Henry IV*. When he's done, I rub my eyes. I can barely keep them open.

"Okay, now I really need to sleep," I say.

"You're not *moved*?"

"I'm moved, I'm moved, but I'm also very tired."

And so we go upstairs, and I sleep in his arms, which is not normally something I like but this time doesn't feel so bad.

I wake up to bright sunlight filtering through my shades. I shift slightly, which wakes him up enough that we are both half asleep and kissing. I go from asleep to craving sex in about ten seconds flat. Soon, he is fingering me and then fucking me and even though I am wide awake, I keep my eyes closed.

"This is all your fault," he says to me, once it's over.

"How is this *my* fault?"

"You sent the text last night. You made the first move. You set off a chain of events the likes of which . . ."

I start to laugh.

"I'm not going to be able to recover from this," he says. "I can't leave here. Where am I going? Seriously, where do I go from here?"

I ask: "Do you feel like playing tennis?" He raises his eyebrows at me.

Soon, he's on the phone with the manager of the Meadow Club, a fancy country club in Southampton. He met him a few weeks ago. Apparently, he's a big Rangers fan.

"All right, we're in," he says. "Get your whites on, sweetheart."

In the car, he's doing nothing but talking trash.

"I am going to smoke you," he says.

"You're not, but it's cute that you think so."

"I don't want to just hit though. Let's play a match. Best two out of three."

"Fine by me."

"I'm going to serve underhand the whole time."

I laugh. "Why? Psychological warfare?"

"You'll see. You're dead."

"I'm more concerned about your self-esteem than anything else."

"My self-esteem? I'm a world-class athlete."

"Oh my god, you're deluded."

"You don't understand. My backhand is not a normal backhand."

"Yeah, yeah. Your backhand is not a normal backhand . . . Your push is not a normal push . . . Spare me the details."

We drive along Gin Lane, pass by the beachfront mansions hidden by hedges. We pull into the Meadow Club, an expanse of forty pristine grass courts and a shingled clubhouse with a green-and-white striped awning. He parks his fancy car in a long row of other fancy cars and it's almost like we belong here. Almost.

We get out of the car. He trails behind me, reaches for my waist.

"You look so hot in that skirt," he says.

I look at him. "This is going to be the easiest match of my life."

The manager greets us at the door to the clubhouse. He shakes our hands and takes us to our court, the court farthest away from the others, the dungeon of the Meadow Club. We're not members. Also, my sneakers have a thin red stripe on them. It's against the rules.

"See what you did," Carter says, shaking his head. "I wanted this match to be on full display."

"Trust me. It's for the best."

During the warmup, we are very cordial. We hit without a lot of pace, straight down the middle of the court. Nobody ventures a winner. Nobody makes a mistake. We say "nice shot" and "good try." We comment on the weather, the quality of the court, the view of the water. It is all very civilized. He comes to net to hit a few volleys and I'm a little thrown off by how large he is. I'm used to playing women.

We take some practice serves. I admire his body as it bends and twists to hit the ball in the air. It really is quite nice. But it can't beat me.

We begin the set. I'm a little nervous because I want to win, and I want to win big. He has a few good shots, but most of his balls are sailing long. I head out to a quick 3–0 lead, just by keeping the ball in the court. He gives me compliments on my shots.

"You're better than I thought you'd be," he says. "Based on your legs."

"What's wrong with my legs?"

"Nothing. Beautiful. But, you know, not super tough."

I nearly lose the last game but take the set 6–0. He throws his racquet. I pump my fist, and then start to laugh. "Sorry. I'll give you a game or two in the next set. I just really wanted that bagel. I wanted to send a message."

He rolls his eyes. "Message received."

The longer we play, the better I feel, the cleaner and more powerful my shots become. It is hard for me to contain myself, hard to not run around a short lob to my backhand side and hammer it as a forehand winner across court. So I do. Over and over again. His backhand may be good, but mine is not even necessary.

Once a game goes to deuce, I don't exactly let him have it, but my play becomes a bit friendlier. I want him to get on the board. And he almost earns it. It's 4–1.

He keeps trying to get me to come up to the net with excuses. He wants to tell me something. He wants a water break.

"This time I just wanted to touch you," he says.

I look around and push him away. "I know. But it's distracting, and it's . . . " He pulls me in, and I shimmy away from his grasp. " . . . not going to work."

But it does. I am being friendly again, playing like I did in the warm-up. I make a few errors.

"I thought you were some big tennis player," he yells from the baseline. "What happened? You lost it?"

I walk up to the service line, and shrug dramatically. "The thing about tennis is . . . sometimes, when you play with somebody much worse than you are, it makes you worse."

He laughs.

I hit the net a few times. I start to curse. It's 4–4. I throw my racquet in disgust. I gather myself and the next two games are a bit of a battle, but I win it. He curses so loudly that they turn toward us four courts over.

"Tough break," I say, shaking my head and smiling as I come to the net. "How's your ego?"

"Bruised. Very badly bruised."

"Well, *I* had a *fantastic* time," I say, as we walk toward the clubhouse. We return the balls and thank the manager. He wishes Carter luck in the new season.

As we head to Carter's car, we see a man who looks familiar to me, but I can't quite place him. He eyes Carter, and then I realize it. I feel a pain in my stomach. It's the man from Tutto. He is with a woman, presumably his wife, and they are dressed in white, crossing the parking lot, headed to their court. He stops walking when he sees Carter.

He smiles at him. "Carter Hughes. Good to see you again. I'm afraid we haven't been properly introduced," he says. He turns to his wife. "Honey, this is Jim's new rookie on the Rangers."

Carter shakes their hands, solemnly.

"How was the helicopter ride to Oyster Bay? Always a fun experience. Your first time. Beautiful home, isn't it?"

"Yeah. It was."

The man turns to me and introduces himself, then says: "I'm sorry, who's this?"

I stick out my hand. "Jessica Riley."

"Jessica Riley . . . That seems easy enough to remember." He has a funny look on his face, a delight that's visible in his eyes. He says: "How do you two know each other? Did you meet at the club?"

"This place?" I laugh a little, to diffuse the tension. "No. This is a tennis club. And Carter doesn't play tennis. He just proved that to me."

The wife is the only one who laughs. The man doesn't flinch. I turn to Carter, but he doesn't break the expression on his face.

"I'm a bit of a novice myself," the wife says. She is wearing a white dress with a white cable-knit sweater draped around her shoulders. Her hair is held back by a large, white bow and she has diamond studs in her ears.

"Well, you look great," I reply, holding up my hands. "And that's half the battle out here."

She asks: "Why don't we all play doubles sometime?"

"Yeah. Yeah. We should," I say, slowing backing away from them. *I'd love to beat the brakes off both of you.* "Well, we're starving . . . Worked up quite an appetite chasing all those balls on the neighboring courts . . . Nice to meet you!"

Carter is silent as we get in the car.

"Well, I guess he survived," I say, buckling my seatbelt. "I didn't see any bandages."

"Yeah."

"I got a little worried when he asked about us."

He doesn't reply.

"What's wrong?"

"Nothing," he says. But something is certainly wrong.

I say: "Maybe going out in public wasn't such a great idea."

He grunts. "You think?"

"It was *your* idea to come here! I wanted to break into one of the homes on our street, which was a much more practical idea."

He is silent.

I say: "And when did you take a helicopter to Oyster Bay?"

"A few days ago. It was nothing."

He starts the engine and pulls out of the spot fast, then hits the brake a little hard. We jerk forward and back. We drive by the courts and away from the club.

I can feel a sadness slowly creeping in, but I'm not ready for it yet. I look out the window at the blue sky, the manicured hedges, one sprawling mansion after another hiding behind them. I want to stay in fantasy land.

I ask: "So you want to get something to eat?"

"Yeah," he says, and puts his hand on my knee. "Where do you want to go?"

"Oh, I don't know. Tutto?" I say, and then I curl up in the seat laughing. I can't stop.

He tries hard not to smile. "Fuck off."

17

CARTER

We're in JT's Toyota, heading west on the Long Island Expressway. It's six o'clock in the morning and for some reason I'm wearing a suit. I texted Jessica a picture earlier.

Just wanted you to see me in real clothes, I wrote.

SHARP, she wrote back.

Finally, the Manhattan skyline appears, like a sphinx rising from the ashes of Queens. I think about everything I'm going to say to the press:

It's the city that never sleeps. The most famous arena in the world.

I'm going to cause a lot of disturbance, go to the net hard, and hit everything that moves. No reins.

I'm going to play with an edge, and no place has more edge than New York City.

I'm ready to go.

But now that it's happening, I'm wondering if I actually am. I'm not sure how I'll do, if I'm well suited for it. It's not how I grew up, not what I'm used to. I'm not sure internal chaos flourishes in external chaos. But as a wise man once said: Fake it till you make it.

JT and Harps don't have to be there with me, but they're along for the ride, eager for a change of scene. They drop me off at the NHL offices on Ninth Avenue. It's Media Day, which takes place every year in New York City, a week before training camp begins, and there is a lot of pageantry going down on the street. I weave through the crowd to meet some communications girl with a headband and black pants on. I follow her into the offices. It's sort of like the first day of school.

Inside, it's a montage of wintry colors that mimic the gray of skate blades and the white of ice. A large, illuminated NHL medallion of polished steel sits at the reception area. There are blurred black-and-white action shots everywhere. Game footage is projected onto one wall. A crystal slab has an etched image of the Stanley Cup, surrounded by plaques with the names of winning players and teams. I go from one conference room to another, answering questions, participating in skits.

Somebody has played a "prank" on me by rolling up my equipment, taping it together and hanging it from the ceiling. I am instructed to walk into the fake locker room and fake surprise. In another room, I bounce pucks off my stick until my forearms are shot. I give choreographed high-fives to guys I've never met before.

"Laugh like I just told you the funniest thing in the world!" a woman behind a camera tells me. Next I have to draw a picture of a hockey rink blindfolded. I text a photo of my finished work to Jessica: *They made me draw this with a blindfold on. Should I bring the blindfold back to the Hamptons with me?*

She replies: *Keep your head in the game.*

We have lunch at the food trucks lined up out front, lobster rolls and cheesesteaks. After, I go back inside and shoot promos with a studio backdrop. I wear my jersey in a fake stall. I pretend to tie my skates and tape my stick and look up at the camera. I sign six hundred posters, bobbleheads, and jerseys. I talk to a few players on other teams, guys I've looked up to, but every interaction is quick. Matthew Tkachuk introduces himself to me.

"Nice to meet you," he says. Nice to meet you. My hero. No big deal.

I leave the building on a high, feeling positively jazzed. And to top it all off, there is a car waiting to take me to my brand-new apartment.

Did I ever have any doubt? No. I'm ready to go.

I meet the driver who is going to take me down to Tribeca. His name is Manny. He's slightly overweight, wearing a white dress shirt and track pants.

"I've been working for Mr. Howard for sixteen years," he says. "I started in the garage. I run all the transportation for MSG. Welcome to New York!"

I get in the car. He deliberately passes by Madison Square Garden, slows down in front.

"There it is," I say.

Manny seems to know everything about the city, and how to get around traffic. There is something about him that is calming.

We head downtown on Seventh Avenue, driving through Chelsea and the Village. We cross Houston Street, then Canal.

"Do you know why it's called Tribeca?" he asks me.

"No," I reply. "Why?"

"It's short for 'triangle below Canal Street.' This area forms a triangular shape between Canal, West Street, and Broadway."

"Tribeca, huh?" I nod and stare out the window. *This is home?*

"Welcome home!" Manny says, as the car pulls onto North Moore Street, up to an industrial building with arched windows. By coincidence, it's called the Ice House.

I get in the elevator, press PHA. I unlock my door, like I'm about to open a present. I'm amazed at what I see. A huge loft with high ceilings and large windows and exposed brick walls. I have three bedrooms. I am king of the world.

JT and Harps are there, reporting about their day, marveling at the city.

"We clocked twenty thousand steps, walked everywhere," JT says. "We had lunch in Soho, went to the World Trade Center. You name it, we saw it."

"There were T-shirts on Canal Street with your name and number on the back. We got you one." Harps throws it at me. I catch it.

They sit on my couch. I take my suit jacket off and throw it on a chair.

"What should we do tonight?" JT asks.

"Already taken care of," I say, and sit down.

"What's that mean?"

"I talked to the guy."

"What guy?"

"There's a promoter. He's in charge of taking care of the players on the team. He's picking us up at 7:30 for dinner."

JT looks at Harps and then back at me. He shrugs. "That makes it easy."

"All right, gentlemen. We're going to start the night at a sushi place called Zero Bond," says the promoter, Adam, who gets out of a black car to shake our hands. He's a slick-looking guy who speaks quickly. He is wearing a black T-shirt and reeks of cologne and looks like he might have played baseball in high school.

In the car, he explains: "The mayor of New York dines here regularly. It's a gathering spot for leaders in business, media, politics, sports. You have to apply and pay six thousand dollars a year to become a member."

"There's an *application?*" I ask. "To eat dinner?"

He explains: "They're looking for some combination of art-kid cool and nightclub sleaze and Hollywood glitz and banker-bro capital."

"Who fits *that* criteria?" I ask.

"Taylor Swift, Gigi Hadid, Kim Kardashian . . ."

"Geez. Suddenly I feel underdressed."

He looks me over. "You're fine. I made sure of that. The dress code is 'smart casual with a New York edge.'"

"I don't know what that means."

He checks his reflection in the rearview mirror. "That's what I'm here for."

We get out of the car on a quiet cobblestone street with

scaffolding covering most buildings. The door has no sign or awning. It's black with the number "0" on it.

The woman at the entrance desk checks names and pushes a button that opens the elevator, which goes straight to a fifth-floor loft space that looks more like an apartment than a restaurant. There is a living room and a library.

We eat rock shrimp and sashimi and spaghetti with caviar, seated on gray suede seats arranged in low clusters. Partitions are set up between the tables, for privacy. The dim lights overhead look like long black matchsticks with golden bulbs at the end.

I text Jessica: *I'm at Zero Bond. Have you been?*

I read her response under the table: *No, but that's a real scene. You'll be a changed man soon.*

Everyone around me is conspicuously good-looking. I catch the eye of a girl at another table, a beautiful brunette with sultry eyes. She is wearing what appears to be a black suit jacket with nothing underneath. She smiles at me.

I ask the waiter for the check, and Adam intercepts me. "There is no check," he explains. "Hope you guys enjoyed yourself," the waiter replies, clearing our plates.

"Okay then," JT says. "If it's free, then it's for me. Where are we going now?"

"Paul's Baby Grand," Adam replies.

"That's the name of a place?" I say.

"Paul's Baby Grand Piano. Sometimes called Paul's. Sometimes Baby. It's a cocktail lounge in a hotel. The owner is a legendary nightclub guy. It's known for its tough door. They can be pretty rigorous, but obviously we'll be fine."

"Obviously," JT says, fully enjoying himself now.

We get into another black car and emerge ten minutes later. On the way into the lounge, Adam introduces me to the bouncer, whose name is Disco. He tells me he's a Rangers fan.

"Disco is incorruptible," Adam tells me. "He has such a good sense of, like, who's going to add to the room and who's just going to suck the energy out of it."

Disco says: "Listen, I'm here to help. You're going to have a lot of questions. Just bring them to me. I'll keep it safe."

I nod. *What questions?* I'm quite sure I've been to a nightclub before.

Inside, it's a tropical-printed oasis. Neon pink walls, a black-and-white checkerboard floor, palm tree lamps.

"Paul's has a finger on the pulse of what it means to be cool," Adam says. "There are different cliques of regulars: international people, celebrities, influencers, the gay nightlife mafia. It's a small ecosystem that represents the culture of downtown. It's like a dysfunctional family." He laughs. "There's a loosely enforced 'no photo' rule, but don't worry. They just have to say that, because if a place *doesn't* have that, it's like saying: 'We don't get A-listers.'"

Adam introduces me to Paul himself, the owner of the bar, who tells me he grew up in Rye and played hockey until he was twelve. He's a diehard Rangers fan. He says I'm welcome back anytime.

I see the girl from the restaurant is here, in the corner, surrounded by an entourage of people.

"Is she famous?" I ask Paul, lifting my chin in her direction.

Paul laughs. "Fame. Fame. What is fame? That's Ella Shay. She's a pop star. She's Canadian, actually, so she probably knows how to skate. You should go say hi."

I get another drink and then go over.

"Heard you used to skate to school," I say.

She smiles. "And where did you get this information?"

I learn that she lives in the West Village and is hosting *SNL* in a couple of weeks. I nod along, finishing off my vodka rocks.

"Don't worry. My brother used to play junior hockey. I know how hockey players drink . . . " she says, eyeing my glass.

She gives me instructions about navigating nightlife in New York as people spill drinks on themselves while dancing on top of the couches.

"Silo is a must, but not on Mondays. Somewhere Nowhere if you're looking for a view. Nebula can be a little touristy, but I don't mind it, especially if Sabrina is DJ-ing. But not before one A.M. Electric Room is small, but fun. Don't go after midnight, though, because it turns into a total zoo . . . "

We watch the staff hang up a disco ball at three A.M. to the instrumental interlude of a Blondie song. The room is spinning.

She cups the back of my neck and says, "Do you want to get out of here?"

I say: "Sure."

"Let's take the subway!" she insists.

"The subway?"

"Yeah! It'll be a trip."

"I've never taken the subway before," I say.

"Don't worry. I'll protect you."

On the platform, she explains that there'll be four stops. I stare at her downturned eyes, the black strap of her purse strewn across her bare chest and collarbone, as she shows me a map on her phone. "And then we'll be in the West Village!" she says.

"Well, what do ya know," I say, and the vodka has done me in just enough to add: "Can I kiss you now or do I have to wait four stops?"

I wake up at Ella's apartment. It smells like flowers, and the inside of a store that sells beautiful, expensive things. I've never seen an apartment like this. From the bed, I see vintage skis and an orange blanket in a bucket by the fireplace. There is a red-painted canvas on the opposite wall that is graffitied with the words: WELCOME ALL BELIEFS SAFE HERE. The night table is a stack of old books with a lamp and a candle on top. It's homey and colorful, quirky and filled with art. A place that would be fun to explore. But I can't do that. Because I feel awful. Like a tidal wave is coming.

Ella is still asleep, enwrapped in her white bedsheets, her bare foot and anklet, a gold chain with a tiny gold key attached to it, the only visible part of her.

I check my phone. I have thirty-seven texts.

JT writes: *Where are you? Have you seen this on Deuxmoi?*

It is a screenshot of an Instagram post. A photo of Ella and me on the train. There is a link to a *New York Post* article: *Ella Shay Spotted with Rangers Rookie Carter Hughes. Why She Needs to Look Out NOW.*

I feel my stomach drop.

I click on the link. *The pop singer and soon-to-be Rangers star appear giddy, but can she tame this hotheaded bachelor? Nobody could deny that they make a beautiful couple . . . but what you don't know . . . He played hockey at the University of New Hampshire, but was almost thrown off the team . . . starting fights . . . propensity for violence . . . arrested for an altercation with three guys . . . Cops were called . . .*

I let my eyes go out of focus. I can't read any further.

I text JT: *You guys drive back. I'll meet you out there.*

I have to get back to the Hamptons immediately. I can't let this bake for two hours while I sit in traffic on the LIE. That would be torture.

I click on the Blade app and book a 7:25 helicopter, then take a cab to the 30th Street heliport. I text Jessica on the way: *Hey, are you awake?*

She doesn't respond. I keep telling myself: *Jessica doesn't check Deuxmoi. Jessica doesn't read Page Six.*

The truth is—I don't know what I'm doing with Jessica. I don't understand why I feel this way now. I'm not even sure whether to feel guilty. All I know is that I have these urges for her that feel overwhelming. I think about her all the time. I can't hurt her without feeling very uncomfortable with myself.

Once I land in East Hampton, I try to get an Uber, but there aren't any available. In the parking lot, there is a lone Crown Vic with the words *East Hampton Town Taxi* written on it. I get in.

The driver is an elderly woman who is confused the whole ride, doesn't have GPS, seems to have never been to the Hamptons, or in a car, before.

"I used to be a flight attendant," she tells me, before making several wrong turns. She is driving at twenty-five miles per hour. Apparently, I am her first passenger, and I am writhing with anxiety as she embarks on this new career.

Forget my checkered past, I am going to get arrested for the murder of this woman. Inform Page Six.

Once she pulls off 27, she starts going even slower. Twenty-five miles per hour was her highway speed. We are a few turns away from our street, and I can't take it anymore. I get out of the car and run.

Jessica answers the door in shorts and a sweatshirt.

I am gasping for air.

"What did you do? Run here from the city?" she asks.

I walk into her house. "She didn't mean anything to me!" I say, halfway keeled over.

She laughs. "What are you talking about?"

"I assume you saw the thing . . ."

"What thing?"

I am pointing at the air. "The thing . . . online."

"Sit down," she says, and then gets a glass of water. I sit at her kitchen table. She hands it to me. "Drink this."

It is silent. I stop talking. I collect myself. She looks at me. "I saw it."

"And?"

"*And* . . . I'm married! I don't want to be involved in some kind of Deuxmoi love triangle with a Canadian pop star! You're going to fuck all these girls! You don't even know what you're doing!"

"So you don't care?"

"Of course I care! I cried for an hour! What did you think?"

"You did?"

"Carter." She pauses, looking down. "I cried for the same reason you ran here."

"Oh."

"I feel exactly like you'd think I would! I feel exactly like *you'd* feel if you heard I'd fucked the gardener!"

"What gardener?"

"I could have a gardener."

"That I've never seen?"

"Some of the best gardeners remain out of sight."

"I don't even like the *mention* of a gardener that you might be fucking."

"See?"

I say, "I didn't fuck her."

She holds up her hand. "Stop. I don't want to know."

"I woke up this morning and all I could think about was you."

She furrows her brows. "I doubt that, but it's okay."

"Is it? I don't know what the rules are here." I put my head in my hands. "I'm so confused."

"Look. This is life. Not everything is so black and white." She sits down across from me and pulls her knees up to her chest. She sighs. "I probably shouldn't have married Alejandro. I probably shouldn't have married . . . anyone. I don't really believe in marriage, and not just because my parents got divorced when I was ten . . . which is apparently the most traumatic age for your parents to get divorced, in terms of awareness and vulnerability . . . but also because *I'm not an idiot.*" She rolls her eyes. "By all means, print up the invitations and have the beautiful ceremony and invite everyone to watch but don't tell me having sex with the same person for a hundred years makes any fucking sense because I won't believe you."

"So why did you do it?"

"Because I fell for it too! Because when a man you love kneels in the street, in the snow, in a suit, in front of the Plaza, and asks you to marry him, you say yes." She smiles. "Believe me. For an investment banker to ruin a perfectly good suit, he must be madly in love. And he was. We both were. So you say *yes*, let's do it. You say *yes*, let's hope for the best."

"And now?"

Her eyes well up with tears. "I think you should go."

"That's it? That's your solution? Are you serious?"

"*Go.*"

I remain sitting. She waits. I stand. She pushes my body toward the door.

"You gotta go. This has already gotten way out of control. Out before I call the police and tell them you're trespassing. And with your track record, they'll believe me."

Maybe because she is physically pushing me out. Maybe because she's crying, or because I'm about to, I leave.

18

JESSICA

As soon as he leaves my house, I look around with a rising sense of panic.

I have to get the fuck out of here.

My plan was to leave three days from now, on Sunday, to spend the next few days crafting the last chapter of my novel, but I can't wait until then. Once I decide, once I say these words to myself, the actions follow swiftly and automatically. I check the train schedule. It's ten in the morning and the next train is at 3:05. *3:05? Seriously?* The weekday schedule is so limited. I'm beside myself that I have to wait until then.

I decide to focus on household chores. I empty my dirty laundry into the washer. I get my suitcase. I pull my clothes from the closet and dump them in the suitcase, unfolded.

I go through the house, room by room, and put everything back in its place, as far as my memory serves. Each part of the house brings some moment with Carter back to me. Each part reminds me of a different chapter. I dust. I vacuum. I shift the clothes from washer to dryer.

It takes a surprisingly short amount of time to wipe the whole slate clean. And I mean clean. I am scrubbing countertops and mopping floors and taking out the garbage. I don't want to leave a single sign of myself here. I'm convinced that the more pristine this environment looks, the less bad that could have taken place.

I eat whatever leftovers are in the fridge for lunch and text Alejandro that I'm going to take the 3:05 P.M. train home.

Today? I thought you were staying until Sunday?

Nope. I'm done. I miss you guys.

We miss you too.

So, if you're having an affair with the babysitter, now would be a good time to end it, I somehow have the audacity to add.

He writes back: *Glad you warned me.*

I smile. Okay. This is good. This is me getting back on track. I call my agent to discuss the details of leaving the house.

"I'm supposed to set the alarm, right?" I ask.

"Yes. Do you remember the code?"

"I think so . . . We'll find out. What about the car?"

"Can't you drive it into the city?"

"I can if you never want to see me again."

"Right. Well, just leave it there then, in the garage. Take an Uber to the train station. Or the Jitney?"

"I'll take the train. This way I don't have to deal with traffic, and I can work."

He laughs. "You're not going to work on the train. You're

going to stare at all the strangers and try to imagine what their lives are like and whether they're happy."

"No. No. I've been alone in the wilderness for months. I'm no longer interested in other people's lives."

"You've changed."

"Sadly, I think I have."

"Well, I can't wait to read the book."

"Yeah! I'm excited to show you. It's almost done. Ninety percent. Just haven't written the ending. But . . . I think it'll come to me when I least expect it, like when I'm in the shower or something. You know what they say about creativity . . . how you have to sit in one place and work really hard and then release it into the universe and then walk away and *then*, and only then, will it come back to you . . . or something."

"Who says that?"

"Don Draper."

"Ah, yes. The source of all your career wisdom."

After lunch, I swim my last laps and then throw my wet bathing suit into the dryer. I do one last scan of every room, the area around the pool. Partially hidden in the crevice of a patio chair, I see his sweatshirt. I feel suddenly frozen in place.

Fuck. What am I supposed to do with this? Leave it on his doorstep? Take it with me? Throw it in the garbage? Fuck. Fuck. Fuck. The stress of this decision causes me to cover my face with my hands. *All right. Come on, Jessica. You're not a teenage girl. Just hide all the evidence and move on.*

I go to the bathroom to splash some water on my face and then I sit on the floor. The bathroom floor is where I always go to do my serious thinking. Something about being on the ground, the cold, hard ground. I wait for the storm to pass over me. *When I leave this house, I am leaving it all behind. When I leave this house, I am going to be a better person, a more giving wife, a more present mother.* I focus on the lonely moments that I've had here, the regretful ones, and then I peel myself off the floor and call an Uber.

As we drive away, I feel like a weight has been lifted. *That house.* That house has been the problem all along. I won't do anything bad ever again so long as I never step foot in that house. I look at pictures of my children the whole ride to the train station, watching the videos of them at the playground yesterday. I just watched the videos last night, but now I watch them more carefully, as if they are a precious commodity, as if they are the only ones I have. I miss their voices the most. When I talk to my daughter on the phone, she sounds older.

On the platform, I wait with the others. There are very few people going back to the city now. It's the Thursday before Labor Day. Everyone out here is here to stay. The people that stand with me seem as agitated as I am, and I wonder what situation they are fleeing from. A husband with an unexpected "meeting" in the city? A houseguest who slept with somebody's wife? The Sunday crowd is different from this. The Sunday crowd is tanned and calmly getting back to their real lives, beach bags and sun hats resting atop their black suitcases. The Thursday crowd? Fugitives.

Usually, when standing on this platform, I am calmly turning the pages of a book. This time, I am on the run.

It is warm and sunny, but the afternoon has that late August feeling, of the season about to change. I stand on the train platform, wind in my hair, wind blowing at my white skirt and T-shirt, like a woman on the verge.

Then I see Carter jogging up the steps to the platform and I can't quite believe my eyes. I rub them, as if he might be a mirage.

"What are you doing?" I say, once he gets close.

He is out of breath. "So you're just going to fucking *leave* and not say goodbye?"

"We said goodbye!"

"No, we didn't."

The train horn sounds in the distance. "How did you even know I was here?"

"I thought you might pull a stunt like this. And then I heard your luggage in the driveway."

The train comes barreling by us and I hold my skirt down with my hands so that it doesn't blow in the huge gust of wind.

I plead with him. "*Please,* Carter. Don't make this harder than it already is."

He throws his hands up into the air. "I don't like your reasoning. I don't like anything you're doing."

The train stops and the doors jolt open. A few people funnel out onto the platform. My fellow fugitives walk on ahead of me.

"Go home!" I yell at him, over the noise, and then march forward, rolling my suitcase onto the train.

"Fine," he says, following me. "I'll go home. My home is in the city now."

I try to push him off the train, but it doesn't work. He doesn't budge an inch. I give him a begging look.

"So you're going to take the train two hours into the city and then two hours back? For no fucking reason?"

"*Challenge me.*"

"Fine." I keep walking down the aisle, rolling my suitcase

into the middle of the train car. "Enjoy the ride. I'm not sitting with you."

"Oh yes, you are."

"Excuse me," I say, squeezing past someone.

I hear over the loudspeaker: *Train to Jamaica. Next stop: Southampton.*

The train begins to move, and I nearly fall over, but manage to keep my balance. I swing open the door to the next car, with my big suitcase clunking around behind me. It is a hard maneuver. Between cars, it's cacophonous noise. He opens the door behind me.

"WHAT ARE YOU DOING?" he shouts over the sound of the wind, the engine, the wheels gliding against the tracks.

"I'm *trying* to get away from you!"

"What are you going to do then? Miss me for the rest of your life?"

I turn back and yell: "AT FIRST I WAS AFRAID, I WAS PETRIFIED."

"You're mentally ill."

"Are you looking in the mirror when you say that?"

I make my way into the next car, where it's quiet. I am unsure of my plan now and keep having to steady myself as the train jerks me from side to side.

"Go ahead," he says. "Keep going. You don't think I can follow you? You're the one with the giant suitcase bumping into everything like a lunatic."

I stumble to the side and use the top of a seat to steady myself.

"You're going to have to sit down eventually," he says. "I'll wait." We stand across from each other. I am gripping the handle of my suitcase for balance. He has his arms across his chest, staring at me.

"You can sit with me for two hours," he says. "We've done a lot worse."

I sigh. "Fine."

I look around. The train is mostly empty. It is easy to find two spots next to each other. I sit down, next to the window.

This station stop: Southampton. This station stop: Southampton. Next stop: Hampton Bays.

He speaks softly now. "You're acting like this is all my fault. But this isn't my fault," he says. "I got options, babe."

I laugh, and it breaks the tension between us. We sit in silence for a few minutes.

"All right," he says. "So the first thing I want to tell you on this train ride confessional is that you've taught me something."

"Oh yeah? What's that?"

"Apparently, you can find someone *incredibly* frustrating but still be in love with them." He looks at me.

"That's a good lesson to learn."

He says: "Tale as old as time. Girl walks into a guy's house, kicks over his speaker, threatens to call the cops . . . "

"It's a classic."

This station stop: Hampton Bays. This station stop: Hampton Bays. Next stop: Westhampton.

I'm pretending not to care. I'm pretending to be perfectly blasé about this train ride. But in my head, I'm calculating stops. I think it's about twelve. Twelve stops until it's over, until I have to give up this pleasure pain. But I'm not getting out of it before twelve, so I let my body relax a little, unclench my jaw. Eventually, I lean against him. Just twelve stops is all I have.

He puts his hand on my leg, slightly gripping my thigh, and I lean into his shoulder, taking in the smell of his shirt. I put my head against his arm and look out the window, and he pulls my leg slightly toward him, takes it in his hands.

"I don't understand," he says.

I sigh. "What?"

"Why would you tell me that I'm going to fuck all these girls, when I only think about fucking you?"

I pause. "That's true. You *don't* understand. We're in completely different situations. If I left my husband, you'd be happy for five minutes and then you'd be miserable."

"How do you know? How do you know *exactly* what would happen?"

"I just know."

"You don't love me?"

"I didn't say that."

He rubs his face with his hands. "Great."

A middle-aged blonde woman comes up to us. She is holding the shoulder of her young son, who is wearing shorts and a blue jersey with yellow writing. She appears nervous. I sit up straight. Carter lets go of my leg.

"Sorry to bother you," she says. "You're Carter Hughes, right? This is Trevor. He plays under eleven for the Massapequa Penguins."

"Nice to meet you," Carter says. "Who's your favorite NHL player?"

Trevor mumbles something softly. A name I don't recognize.

"Interesting. Okay. Be careful with this one. Who's your favorite Ranger?"

The kid thinks for a minute, then smiles. "Matt Rempe," he says.

Carter laughs. "Well, I hope you have a good practice. Practice hard."

"It's just practice," Trevor says.

The mother rolls her eyes. Carter gets animated.

"No. *No.* It's not just practice!" he says. "It's never just practice! How badly do you want to win?"

The mother and son laugh, thank him, and then leave. Carter turns to me. "Matt Rempe." He shakes his head. "Kid's a psycho."

This station stop: Westhampton. This station stop: Westhampton. Next stop: Remsenburg-Speonk.

There is momentary silence between us. I pull my knees up to my chest, smoothing my skirt on the sides, wrapping my arms around my legs. I look out the window. He sighs and then turns to me. I look at him. I put my feet back down on the ground. He grabs my face and starts kissing me. He pushes me back against the side of the train, until I can feel the cold of the window on the back of my head.

"We really shouldn't be doing this," I whisper, my eyes half closed. "What if somebody sees us?"

"Do you recognize anyone on this train car?"

I look around. "No."

"So then?"

He moves his face closer to mine. I look around one more

time, then pull him toward me by his T-shirt, by the sides of his body.

Soon, we are fully making out, my legs intertwined with his. His hands are up the sides of my bare legs, playing with the edge of my skirt, feeling underneath it.

This station stop: Remsenburg-Speonk. This station stop: Remsenburg-Speonk. Next stop: Mastic-Shirley.

Some drunk kids get on the car. They are talking about a concert they're going to. *It's going to be sick, man. SICK. We're going to have the sickest night.* They break out a tin of tobacco. I can hear them snap it. They start head banging to Metallica. *Give me fuel, give me fire . . .*

They are laughing at us, but we can't break apart for anything. His hands are fully under my skirt now, running his fingers under the seam of my underwear.

"Let's fuck," he whispers in my ear, and then kisses my cheek. "Come on. One last time." He touches the wetness between my legs, through my underwear, then pushes the underwear aside, puts his fingers inside of me. I gasp as quietly as I can, into his ear, then dig my face into the side of his neck, my best attempt at hiding.

I touch the back of his head with my hand and look into his eyes. "I'm not fucking on a train," I whisper, but I can't push him away. I can't tell him to stop what he's doing.

"Who said anything about a train? Let's just get a hotel in Babylon or something . . ."

I laugh. "Oh, I'm sure that would be lovely."

He kisses my neck. "*Please.* Come on."

"No . . . no."

"I need to fuck you one more time."

"It's enough. Enough," I say, putting my head on his chest and my hands under the back of his shirt.

"One more time and then it'll be enough," he says.

My eyes narrow at him. "Do you think so?"

He shakes his head no.

The drunk kids start hollering. One of them has a particularly loud cackle that he keeps doing, just to mess with us.

"Oh, would you *please* shut the fuck up?" I yell at the kids.

One replies: "We're not going to shut up just because some *slut* asks us to."

Carter stands up. "Whoa. Whoa. Whoa. Let's maybe take it down a notch, fellas."

"*You two* take it down a notch!" he yells back. Carter sits down.

"You know something?" I say, laughing. "They're right."

We're getting closer to the city. It's time to get it together. I clear the stray hairs from in front of my face, my mouth, put them behind my ears.

This station stop: Mastic-Shirley. This station stop: Mastic-Shirley. Next stop: Sayville.

A man and a woman get on in matching clothes and start doing a song-and-dance number. They perform something from an opera, then morph into a bad version of Frank Sinatra. They go around asking for money.

I say to Carter: "They should give us money for listening."

He laughs. "Tell them that."

"I'm not going to tell them that!"

"Tell them that you never asked for their song."

"You know, you can't just say whatever you want to people. We live in a society."

"You care way too much about what other people think."

"Maybe you care too little."

This station stop: Sayville. This station stop: Sayville. Next stop: Bellville.

I look out the window, where I can see some houses but mostly trees. You can see almost nothing of these towns from the train. We start making out again, and I am beyond annoyed by the existence of clothes.

This station stop: Bellville. This station stop: Bellville. Next stop: Bayport.

A young girl gets on. She's talking on the phone. She just got into a huge fight with her mom. She's loudly describing how she's going to the city without her. She calls her dad to say: *You won't believe what Mom just did.* She is upset, on the verge of tears.

"I feel so bad," I say. "Someone should talk to her. Should I talk to her?"

"Talk to her?"

"Yeah. I fight with my mom all the time. I know exactly what to say."

"Do not get involved with this random person."

"But her mom sounds terrible!"

"It seems like she knows that."

This station stop: Bayport. This station stop: Bayport. Next stop: Islip.

A guy gets on the train and sits across from us. He starts shaving right there in his seat, throwing shaving cream onto the floor.

"Ugh. Gross," Carter says. "Is he serious?"

I wince. "Maybe he's a homeless guy going to see his family who he hasn't seen in a long time and he's trying to make a good impression."

He laughs. "That's quite a web you're weaving."

This station stop: Islip. This station stop: Islip. Next stop: Babylon.

Babylon is the first station where you can see the outside world. You can see the town. The station is across the street from a high school, a large brick building. You can see the football field. *This station stop: Babylon. This station stop: Babylon. Next stop: Hicksville.* After Babylon, the landscape changes to real suburbia. There are strip malls. It feels like we are finally entering the realm of reality.

This station stop: Hicksville. This station stop: Hicksville. Next stop: Mineola. With every stop, there are bigger crowds coming onto the train. It's clear that we are into the suburban commuter towns.

The city is close.

I feel a sense of sadness in my eyes before I feel it anywhere else. A tingly sensation between my eyes, implying future pain that will be much worse.

How many stops are left? This isn't good.

This station stop: Mineola. This station stop: Mineola. Next stop: Jamaica.

Jamaica is a searing pain to my chest. It went by so quickly. It all went by so quickly. What rolls over me at the exact same time is relief and sadness and the realization that I'll never do it all again.

Jamaica. Trains to Penn Station, Track 1. Next train to Grand Central, Track 2. Atlantic Terminal, Track 7.

Almost the entire train empties out at Jamaica. We walk up the stairs and to the next set of tracks over, then go down the stairs. There are hordes of people waiting on the other track. We maneuver our way through them. My plan was to stop kissing him now. But there are so many people and our bodies are so close. I kiss him quickly, and then look down. "I love you," I say.

"Oh god, please don't do this to me," he whispers back.

The front of the train blows by us. We get on.

Next stop is Penn Station.

There's nowhere to sit, so we stand in the middle of the car. People bump into us and our bodies come together and we try not to lose it. He is holding my hand. His other hand is grazing my hip. We're standing so close and there are so many people that none of this can be seen by anyone.

We get off the train at Penn Station and walk together up into the light, the dimming afternoon light on Eighth Avenue, where we are slowly following the crowd of people in backpacks, shuffling by us on all sides. On the street, horns are blaring. There is a long line of people waiting for taxis. There are greetings and goodbyes all around us. We are not used to being surrounded by this many people. We are moving at a glacial speed.

I look around at Penn Station and Madison Square Garden. I hold my arms out. "This is your new home. I mean . . . office. How cool is that? I'll be watching." I point my finger at him. "Don't disappoint me."

He shakes his head at the ground.

"This can't be it. We're never going to see each other again? I don't believe you."

I shrug, but of course I feel it too. None of this feels real. He comes close to me, kisses the side of my head.

He smiles. "What if you need more material?"

"The book is done!"

"What about the sequel?"

I wave him off and laugh and put my hands on his shoulders. "Enjoy the train ride back to the Hamptons."

"Please. That blade underneath the track might as well be slicing me."

"Hey. Maybe there will be some cute girl . . . on the train . . . waiting to tell you that she just *loves* hockey . . ."

"If she's not antagonizing me, I'm not interested."

We hug one last time and I whisper his name into his ear, and he says mine into my hair, and I somehow manage to turn and walk away.

When I open the door to my apartment, everyone is so happy to see me that I almost cry. My daughter has so much to say, so much to show me, that she doesn't stop talking for twenty minutes straight. She won't allow Alejandro to talk to me at all. I listen to her while silently reorganizing the apartment. I adjust the furniture and lamps slightly, put the mail into a neat pile, throw out the junk. I fluff everybody's pillows and comforters and wipe down the handle of the fridge.

My daughter tells me that she taught her brother how to say the word *trajectory*. She says it to him, asks him to repeat. He does, somewhat successfully.

"Wow! That's a fancy word," I say, laughing.

I ask her about her new soccer class that she is taking with her friend Ashley.

"I had so much fun! I scored *seven* goals today!"

"Wow! Was Ashley there? Did she have fun too?"

"She was there, but she didn't have fun."

"Why not?"

"She was the goalie."

Alejandro is busy working on a pitch that will happen first thing in the morning, and I've been gone for a million years in parenting time, so I'm in charge of dinner and turn-down service tonight.

I order three types of pasta from an Italian restaurant in our neighborhood. I cut the meatballs into tiny pieces. It all comes back to me like riding a bike.

I give baths. I persuade my daughter, who is hysterical about a tiny cut on her finger, that it's okay if her Band-Aid falls off in the bath. We have more Band-Aids in the kitchen. They are unicorn themed. All will not be lost.

I shimmy pajamas onto their damp bodies. I attempt to put on a car show for my son. I listen to him say, "Not this one" a bunch of times. I'm not up on which one is the right one, with the right cars, making the right noises. After I turn off the TV, I sit in his room while he mimics the sound of an ambulance until he passes out.

I go into my daughter's room. She's in tears, anticipating scary dreams.

"Scary dreams happen," I say. "I have them sometimes. But they aren't real. Monsters aren't real. Think about it. Have you ever seen a monster? They might stay hidden for a while, but eventually they'd get hungry, and you'd see them in restaurants.

"Think about something else. Think about something happy, and then your dreams will be happy."

"I checked the closet! I checked under the bed! There's nothing there! Yes, I'll keep the door open. No, I won't shut it. I won't. I won't. Even after you fall asleep."

She lets me leave. She calls me in again. She says: "I know I'm really annoying and you want me to go to sleep, but my brain has so many questions and I won't remember them in the morning."

"Okay," I say, sitting on her bed. "Go ahead."

Once she's out, I find Alejandro in his office.

"I am awash in stress," he says, turning from his computer to look up at me.

"Why? You do this all the time!"

He sighs. "I just really want this one. There are three other banks competing, but I really, really want it."

"Are you almost done? Do you want me to wait for you to go to bed?"

"No," he says. "Go ahead. I still have a lot to do."

I finish unpacking. I eat leftover pasta. I read. I watch TV. In the stillness, the dark, the quiet of my bedroom, I allow my thoughts to drift. I replay the train ride, in its entirety, because I can't help myself.

The waves still hit me here, miles from the ocean, but I feel safe.

I take a shower. When I get out, I stare at myself in the mirror, at my body wrapped in a towel. I can see my tan lines, the white lines where my bikini top once lay. They are fading already. I put on a T-shirt and my sexiest black underwear. I go back into Alejandro's office and lean against the door frame. He looks me over and smiles.

"Can I help you?" he asks.

"You should take a break. Clear your head. It'll be good for you. You always say you do a better presentation when we've had sex the night before."

"Yeah. That's true. But . . ."

"Come on." I narrow my eyes at him. "How badly do you want to win?"

After it's over, Alejandro goes back into his office, and I go into the living room and turn on my computer. The screen is the only thing illuminating the room. I am processing all these conflicting emotions, and yet I feel a sense of calm wash over me as I type.

How do I reconcile all of this? I'm not the same person that I was the last time I sat at this computer. I'll never be the same again. But I guess maybe that's exactly how I reconcile it. I was changed by him. And I'll never be the same again. Who needs the old Jessica? Seriously. Who needs her?

Still, I'm not okay. Not yet, anyway. I'm sad, and a little lonely, in a way that I never was before I left. It's hard to get comfortable with people coming and going. Of course, the going is worse, especially the ones that hit hard, that you can't imagine you'll ever go without. Then again, maybe there is something to being tied to someone, to the consequences if you leave. Maybe I do believe in marriage after all. Maybe it's not nonsense. Maybe it's just hard.

People always ask me why I don't wear my wedding ring.

And I always lie. I say it's too fancy, too tight, or just none of your damn business. But the truth is: I don't wear it because I use my hands to write, and when I look down at my hands on the keyboard, clicking away, I want them to be free. Here, I have a little barrier between myself and the outside world. Here, I have a space to call my own. So I sit there, in the dark, and I write the ending to my book, and for the moment, I feel free.

19

CARTER

It's late by the time I get back to the Hamptons. I see my lone car in the dark at the train station and get a leaden feeling. I go to sleep with that sensation still lingering, like I took a stupid penalty in the third period and cost my team the game.

In the morning, everyone is all business. The business of enjoying the last weekend of the summer. For the next three days, Harps and JT drag me to barbecues and beach bonfires and house parties. I attend all these events in a fog, while the guys make their final rounds.

They make it look easy. They came, they saw, they conquered. Meanwhile I see Jessica wherever I go. This phantom image of her sitting on the beach, ordering a drink at the bar, appearing in a crowd at a party.

Everyone is relaxed and happy and talking about their summer fatigue, their mixed feelings about the change of season. *I'm sad that summer's over but so ready to get back to the city!* say a hundred different girls. They're sad but excited. Am I excited? Yes, I'm excited. They love to use the word "excited." Yup. I get it. Thrilling.

I know I shouldn't be holding on to her, even in my mind, but it's not easy to stop. I do all right during the day, aside from the occasional memory of how she tastes or smells that briefly turns me on and then plunges me into a depression. But, at night, lying in bed, when everything is quiet, it creeps over my body more completely, this urge to pull her to me, so strong that it feels like she must know. I say things to her that she'll never hear. I have deluded hopes that she'll text me, but she doesn't. That's almost a given.

I type a few messages and then delete them. I think about writing her a letter, and then I think *A letter? Who are you? Have you lost your mind?*

After three days, I adjust to looking at the dark windows of her house. I accept that this house is now empty. I stop trying to think of ways to get her back. I swear her off. She is with her family. She has a *family. She doesn't need you anymore.*

"Nothing ever ends," says Harps, who notices my mood has been progressively sliding off a cliff. *Nothing ever ends, huh? I hate you and every armchair philosopher who has come before you.*

"Thanks," I say.

We're supposed to spend the weekend packing up our house, but Sunday night comes, and nobody has done anything. Instead, it's just getting messier and dirtier, in our final push to close out the summer. Luckily, on Monday morning, I wake up to JT, who has been missing for two days, roaming around the house and rolling on ecstasy. He has cleaned the whole place, from soup to nuts, and is sweating through his shirt, doing some ab workout that involves our patio chairs.

Problem solved, apparently.

The last thing we do is wipe the crayon off the mirror in Harps's room, with all our points written on them.

"Time well spent," says JT. We agree. Declaring a winner is not necessary and a little bit frowned upon.

I'm headed to Manhattan. They're driving to rookie camp in Tarrytown. We say goodbye in the driveway.

"It's been fun, fellas," Harps says, as he takes a bag off the ground and loads it into his trunk. "Thanks for the house, Hughes."

"Yeah," I say. "Thanks for looking after me."

JT shakes my hand and says: "I'd say 'don't change' but honestly, you could use a few tweaks."

I laugh and say to him: "Play hard. Play responsible. Pucks in at the blueline. Pucks out at the blueline."

I turn to Harps: "You'd better own that crease."

Harps replies: "I will." He gives me a nod. "Remember: The sun never sets in the East."

"Right," I say, even though I have no fucking clue what he's talking about.

And then I get into my car and drive, away from them, away from the house, away from our summer. My bags are piled up in the backseat and blocking the view out the back window.

I listen to some jam band radio station for the entire ride back to the city. I turn my phone off.

When I get to my apartment, I dump all my stuff in the corner of the living room. I watch a series of New York movies—*Home Alone 2, Goodfellas, 25th Hour.*

The next morning, I'm out on the street early, in my sweats, headed to get a bagel and groceries, surrounded by parents taking their children to their first day of school. My phone rings. It's my new coach, Mark Murphy.

"Carter. It's Coach."

I put down the items I've picked up at the grocery store, shove them next to an empty spot near the pretzels. I leave the store.

He says: "I heard you're back in town. Why don't we get together today for a burger? Talk about the season. I like to do this with all the guys before training camp starts."

Hours later, I walk from Tribeca to the West Village, occasionally glancing at Google Maps on my phone. I stop once I get to Jane Street, in front of a red brick building with a black door. A square sign says CORNER BISTRO in neon red. The inside is all wood paneled with wooden chairs and green leather bar stools. It's old fashioned, feels like it hails from a different era.

"First time here?" Coach Murphy asks me, as we take our seats. He's fifty-something, but in great shape. Looks hard. Stern. Never takes a day off.

"First time," I say.

"It's an institution. Been here since the sixties."

We eat thick burgers with bacon and American cheese, and he tells me about his love of deep-sea fishing. He eats the burger without the bun. Doesn't touch his fries.

"Carter," he says. "I think you have the ability to someday be the captain of the New York Rangers. Do you want to be the captain someday?"

"I haven't thought about that."

"You need to start thinking about everything."

"Okay."

"Heard you were in the Hamptons," he says.

I nod. I'm suddenly agitated. "Yup. I was in Bridgehampton for the summer."

"I was just in Montauk," he explains. "My wife and I stayed at Gurney's. It was great. A weekend away from the kids. Who were you working out with out there?"

"Harps and JT. They lived with me all summer and we pushed the shit out of each other."

He pauses. "Well, you can't act in the city the same way you did in the Hamptons. You've got a microscope on you, and it just got enlarged. Who you fight, who you fuck, where you buy your groceries . . . it's all going to be documented online."

"I've had some experience with that already."

He stares at me. "That's nothing. Believe me. Everything changes now. And you'll get in a lot less trouble fucking a pop star than a married woman."

Jessica. He knows. Of course he knows.

I stare at him, silent for a moment.

"That's done now."

"Okay, good. Because it's all going to be documented." He goes on: "When you walk around New York City, you've got to act like you're in a Rangers jersey, like you might be the captain of this team someday. Got it?"

"Got it."

"Wherever you go."

"Understood."

"As far as the on-ice behavior goes . . . " He narrows his eyes at me. "I've played a lot of games hungover. I don't care if you're playing for a contract or if you're playing guilty. God knows I've burned the candle hard on and off the ice. But it can't get the best of you or our team."

"Right. Of course."

"I heard your comments to the press about hitting everything that moves . . . But we don't want you to do that. We want you to be selective, to play a certain way. This will all become clear once we get into it at camp."

"I was told no reins?"

He laughs. "There's no such thing as no reins."

I walk down West Fourth with Coach Murphy's words circling around in my head. I'm walking quickly, with purpose. It feels oddly exhilarating, as I take in all the action on the streets. I wind up on the corner of Perry Street and Bleecker, where it looks like the New York of movies—trees lining the streets and ivy-covered brownstones. One of the brownstones has a crowd of tourists taking pictures in front of it. A photoshoot is taking place on the sidewalk, by a store on Bleecker, where a beautiful girl is commanding everyone's attention.

I look closer. Is that Ella? Holy shit. It is.

She's standing with her hair parted down the center, her bangs falling into a pair of sunglasses. She's wearing a T-shirt and a skirt, loafers with white socks. People are fiddling with her hair and makeup.

As the sea of bodies leaves her, she makes eye contact with me. She waves, looks pleased to see me. I'm happy to see her too.

She motions for me to come over, then gives me a hug and a kiss.

"I'm dying," she says. "I've been here since six in the morning."

"Six in the morning?"

"Brutal, right? You know, I thought about you last night. I almost texted." She glances at a crowd standing across the street, holding up their phones in our direction.

"Come with me," she says. She brings me into her trailer.

As soon as the door closes, she grabs my shirt, pulls me toward her, bites my lip.

She laughs. "Oh, shit. Sorry." She takes her thumb and touches my mouth, which is covered in lip gloss. She gently rubs it in. Her eyes are wide, staring at me while she does it.

I pick her up. She wraps her legs around my waist. I take her over to the couch, which is covered in layers upon layers of sweaters. I clear the decks and lay her down and immediately take her T-shirt off, so that her breasts are exposed. I start sucking her tits, as she moans underneath me. Her moans get louder and longer. She arches her back, glances over at the door.

"You have two minutes," she says.

I slide her lace underwear to the side and unbutton my jeans. She grabs my dick. "Oh my god, you're so hard."

I look down at her body. "Where do you want me to come?" I say, and then put my hands on her hips and move inside of her. She lets out a deep moan and then closes her eyes.

Afterward, I watch as Ella reassembles her outfit. I sit on the couch, silently, as she fixes her hair in the mirror. She applies lip gloss and sprays her face with some sort of mist. In a mere moment, she goes from hot and bothered to camera ready. A total pro.

I ask: "So how does it feel to be photographed every day?"

"A bit strange. Sometimes I'll go out in sweatpants and sneakers, and I can't believe they're taking my picture. I'm like, who cares? This is the most boring thing ever." She shrugs. "The most powerful women in the world are famous and photographed."

We hear a knock on her trailer.

"Ella! We need you!"

"One minute!" she replies, then asks me: "So what are you doing for the rest of the day?"

"I'm going to MSG for an equipment fitting, but I've got some time to kill first. I'll walk around."

"Well, you're in the right place! This is the best neighborhood to explore. That's why I live here. You can judge everyone in New York by where they live. Everyone young and cool lives downtown."

"What if you live on the Upper East Side?" I ask, thinking of how Jessica lives there.

She laughs. "The Upper East Side is for moms and widows."

"Yeah. It's a whole different world up there."

"It really is."

I ask her what she's doing after this is over.

She sighs. "Press. I just finished an album." She winces. "It feels weird to say that! Finished. What does that even mean, when it comes to art?"

"What is time?"

"Exactly!" She laughs. "What *is* time?"

She looks at me, smiling. Her eyes are bright. "I have a crazy idea."

"What's that?"

"What are you doing tonight?"

"Tonight?" I think it over. "Nothing . . . I have a few more New York movies to scratch off my list."

She laughs. "I'm going upstate to Woodstock. I have a house there. It's where I wrote all the songs for my album. A bunch of my friends are coming. It'll be mostly music people, and a few of my actor friends. Would you want to come?"

We hear another knock on the door. "ELLA!"

"COMING!" She raises her eyebrows at me.

"Yes," I say. "Fuck it. Let's do it."

"You're a smart man, Carter Hughes," she says, holding my elbow and then sliding her hand down to my wrist. "Text me when you get home later, okay? We'll figure out the details."

She leaves her trailer and tells me to wait a few minutes before leaving.

"I'll distract all the cameras for you," she says.

A few minutes later, I leave the pack of people and cameras and held-up phones, and head uptown. By the time I get to Sixth Avenue, my head is spinning. *Jesus, Carter. Your coach just told you that you might someday be the captain of the Rangers, and then you fucked a famous pop star inside her trailer in the middle of the West Village.* Not a bad couple of hours. I feel like I'm walking two feet off the ground, like after a few days of misery, the clouds have parted and the sky beyond it is blue, blue, blue.

I walk into 4 Penn Plaza and take the elevator down. I pass

through a long hallway with photos lining the walls of famous Garden moments, photos taken by George Kalinsky of Aretha Franklin and David Bowie, of Elvis Presley and Patrick Ewing. I pass by the laundry room, glance at the neatly stacked towels everywhere and jerseys hanging from the ceiling. I take in the faint smell of sweat and blood and fresh laundry. I keep walking until I get to the locker room.

I'm being sized for new skates.

The skates come out of the oven. They're warm and a bit stiff. I lace them up and start the walk that, hopefully, I'll be taking for a long time—from the dressing room to the ice.

As soon as I hear my skates on a new sheet of ice, it's a direct line to my memory. There is a physical and audible imprint that gets set into my body immediately, bringing forth twenty years' worth of data, taking individual points in time, like the first time I skated on outdoor ice, and connecting them.

I'm alone on Garden ice. It is dead silent. I can hear only the sound of my blades. The upper bowl is dark. The lower bowl is lit at fifty percent. I can see shadows in the stands. The only thing fully lit is the ice. It occurs to me that the Garden doesn't feel hollow, even when it's empty. Maybe it's all that energy, baked into the walls over time. Maybe it's the acoustics. A circular temple built underground.

The Garden has great ice. You can feel how well taken care of it is. It feels hard, solid, strong. It has depth, endless layers of whiteness. With some ice, you can see exactly how thick it is. But this is NHL ice, and it ain't cheap.

I skate a few laps and feel lighter. I'm letting go of something, the past maybe. When I skate, I feel in control. I only hear the sounds I want to hear. I like the feel of new skates, how they're very stiff, almost uncomfortable, at first. They're hot when you put them on, but they gradually cool down and mold to your feet. Maybe it's like me and New York. Stiff at first, but we'll come together over time.

As I skate, I replay the warning from Murphy in my head. We're already at odds. Because he wants me to stay within the lines, and I want everyone to know when I'm on the ice. I want this team to be anemic without me. If I miss a few games, I want them to run the stats on the bottom of the screen—with Hughes, without him.

I'm making Cs on the ice with my feet, going in tight circles. I take several long strides. I put more pressure on the front of my blade, then the back. I look up at the ceiling, the rafters, all the banners. This isn't like other arenas. It's unique—the way the roof domes over the ice and becomes part of the building. There are no bad angles, from the ice to the stands, the goal to the penalty box, to our bench, the visiting bench. It's not just a stadium. It's a Colosseum.

I am *ready* for opening night. I want to play right now, to hear people cheering, to see what this place feels like when it's alive. I want to feel the heartbeat of this stadium so badly that I start talking to it.

Okay, baby.
I respect your calmness, your stillness, right now.
But promise me we won't have too many of these moments.
Promise me we won't have too many quiet times like these.
I'm going to put my foot on the gas. I'll keep people in your seats.

I've heard that if you're loud enough, I can actually feel you move.

I promise to always take care of you.

I'm going to let you down sometimes, but we'll get through it.

You'll never be sorry.

If you're not happy, I'm not happy.

Thank you for this moment.

Thank you for all the gifts you're going to give me.

I start to skate a little faster. I feel a sense of freedom, of flying. Anything is possible here, in New York City. I start to picture the faces of people in the stands, the Garden faithful—the bankers, the firefighters, the cops, the teamsters, the families who have taken the train to be here. And then I see Jessica, sitting there in jeans and a sweater, cheering for my team. Our relationship was like my game, an impulse grab with no barriers, no restraint, no holds barred. She's just my kind of teammate.

I keep imagining her, letting the sensation take over. I let myself feel how I would feel if she were sitting there. All thoughts of her that I've pushed away for the past few days come rushing back. I let them loose, let them circle around the rink along with me, in all their glory. It feels safe to let them go here, to let them have one last dance, before I put them away for good.

I think about how nothing she ever says is expected. Expected is not even worth opening her mouth.

Everyone she encounters is either a horrible nightmare or endlessly fascinating.

She is impatient, easily annoyed, quick to fly off the handle, primed for a battle.

Neutral is death to her. Silence is death.

Around and around and around I go, the image of her sitting there watching becoming more real, more intense. I'm picturing a Saturday night game in December. Jessica arrives alone. I score the overtime winner. I shower, put on my suit, and walk out to the Zamboni entrance. It's our designated meetup spot. We like to avoid the wives' room, for obvious reasons. As soon as I see her, I need to touch her, kiss her, feel the inside of her body.

Oh my god, it's Carter Hughes, she says, smiling. *Can I get your autograph?*

How about I give you something better?

I lead her down a hallway, into the laundry room, and I close the door. Nobody can hear us because of the gentle hum of the machines. I press her up against the wall. I say: *God, you smell so good.* I get her naked in seconds, her mouth on mine the whole time.

Two and a half hours is too long, she whispers, her breath hot against my ear. *It's too long to wait.* Her skin is so inviting, soft and smooth and warm, like it's lit from within. My lips are on her shoulder. I'm squeezing her bare ass, moving my fingers between her thighs. Our tongues are snaking over each other. She's wet against my fingers and getting close. She gently touches my forearm, trying to hold out, but she can't quite tell me to stop. Then she finally does it, moves my hand away, spreads her fingers to weave them through mine.

She wants me to get undressed. *Hurry,* she begs. As soon as my clothes are off, my body is back to hers, both bodies flooded with relief, finally getting exactly what they want. Her skin against mine feels electric. I lift her up onto a folding table. I am tracing her hips with my fingers, going between her legs with my tongue. Her body is rocking back and forth. I stop. I say: *Don't come yet*, looking into her eyes.

Her fingers encircle my dick. *I need this in my mouth*, she says. She kneels, slides her tongue up and down, and then she lies down, on her back, on a spread of clean towels.

As soon as I slide into her, I feel everything spinning inside me slow down and click into place. She's so alive in this, even more so than in the beginning, because she's comfortable with me now. She moves my body, shows me exactly where she wants me to be. *Yes,* she says. I hold on until she's ready. I don't want to come without her. I don't want to do *anything* without her.

My arms are wrapped tightly around her back. And then she tilts her head back, and I watch her mouth open and her body tremble. When she calms down, she smiles, gives me a long look, and says: *Try to forget about me. I dare you.*

A horn goes off. I stop skating and look up. In the timekeeper's box, there are two people testing out the scoreboard buzzer. I come back to reality, feel the hole inside of me dig a little deeper. My movements begin to slow. I sit down on the bench and stare down at the floor. *Fuck*.

When I emerge from the underground, Manny is there waiting to take me home. There is an autumn chill in the air. I get in the car and look up at the black sky. Not a star in sight.

"Home, Mr. Hughes?" he asks.

"Yes, please."

"You got it."

He tells me that there's traffic on Seventh Avenue, so he's going to take the West Side Highway to Chambers Street. I don't say anything, just stare out at the lit-up buildings, the hordes of strangers milling about on the sidewalk.

I take my phone out of my pocket. There is a text from Ella: *I just wrapped. On my way home to pack.*

I look up Woodstock. An hour and forty-nine minutes away. I stare at the dark blue line on the map, an almost straight, almost perfect line heading north. Through the car window, I can see the reflection of the city lights. I can see half of my face, looking out, giving up little information about what's going on inside of me.

"Hey, Manny," I say. "Question for you."

"Yes?"

"How long does it take to get from here to the Upper East Side?"

Acknowledgments

Sean would like to thank Leslie for all the early-morning texts and her overall flagrant disregard for the time difference between California and New York, for teaching him about "false notes" and then tolerating all the times he threw it back in her face. For not getting overly offended when he started calls with "I need a cigarette before talking to you" and ended them with "Can I go now?"

When I said, repeatedly, "My brain is melting," I meant it in a good way.

Leslie would like to thank Sean for teaching her that "waxed" is a combination of drunk and high, for all the calls urging her to include the concepts of "danger" and "texture" and "scent." For the max-volume words of encouragement and sometimes just a video of a finger being severed by a skate. For all the heated discussions about life, love, sex, lip gloss, and whether you remove a strapless top by going up or down.

ACKNOWLEDGMENTS

I could not have written this book without you, even though I told you that I could, a lot of times.

Collectively, we'd like to thank:

Ian Kleinert, Richie Kern, Glenn Yeffeth, Leah Wilson, Elizabeth Smith. Shelly Kellner, David Siffert, Shira Jaffe, Jess Spitzer, Mariel Grossman, Lauren Betesh, Katie Night, Marc Eskenazi, Andrea Bacher, Jen Lavoie, Yulia Kostadinova, Ellen Fedors, Lucy Peck, Michael Seidel, Andrew Blauner, David Duchovny. David Verbitsky, Jean Cohen, Mark Cohen, Diane Cohen, Allison McEneaney, Danny McEneaney, Phillip Rosen.

Marlene Avery.

Hockey moms everywhere.

You know what you did.

About the Authors

Sean Avery was born in Toronto, Canada. He played twelve seasons in the NHL and retired as a New York Ranger. His first book was his best-selling autobiography, *Ice Capades*. He has since transitioned to acting and was in the Academy Award–winning movie *Oppenheimer*. He lives in Laurel Canyon, California. His favorite band is Phish.

Leslie Cohen is the author of *This Love Story Will Self-Destruct* and *My Ride or Die*. She studied literature and creative writing at Columbia University. She lives on the Upper West Side with her husband and two children. Her favorite hockey team is the New York Rangers.